CW01498084

BEYOND THE BLUE LINE

KELLY MOORE

Illustrated by
DARK WATER COVERS

Kelly Moore

TITLE

BEYOND
THE
Blue line

BEST SELLING AUTHOR
KELLY MOORE

PLAYLIST

Hold On by Brandon Ray and Lauren Weintraub
   It'll Be Okay by Rachel Grae
   Think I'm Gonna Love You by Michael Leah
and Caleb Hearn
   I'll Be There For You by Brent Morgan
   Give Into Me by Garrett Hedlund and Leighton
Meester
   Where You Belong by Matt Hansen
   Different Lives by Fly By Midnight
   Enough of Me by Rachael Grae
   Author by Jacob Lee

1 PIPER

Summit Ridge, Montana, is as cold as an Eskimo's butt, although I've never experienced the chilliness of an Eskimo's derrière, I can only assume it's pretty chilly. The ground is so frozen that if it had a breath, it would puff out white clouds of icy air. The people that I pass on the street - crazy there are so many - stroll around with their cups of Joe, treating minus ten degree weather like it's a light breeze. Meanwhile, here I am, daydreaming about my warm, heated blanket and fuzzy, gray hippopotamus slippers, trying not to become a human popsicle.

Who knew sunlight could be so blinding off mounds of snow? There's so much white stuff, I'm tempted to belt out the classic *White Christmas* tune where Bing Crosby and Danny Kaye are sitting on the train with the Haynes sisters on their way to Vermont. "Snow, snow, snow," I croon an off-tune performance, earning a confusing look from a passerby. Bing Crosby is probably doing somersaults in his grave.

"If you unleash that singing prowess again, Piper, the cops will personally escort you back to Harmony Grove with a 'Do Not Return' sticker on your forehead," Maggie cackles so loud, I fumble my cell phone.

"Hey, I thought you were my number one fan, cheering for my future signing contract," I protest.

"Piper, when you sing, even the shower-head begs for mercy," she quips.

"Harsh, Maggs! Are you implying I should abandon my showbiz dreams?" My raised brow is seriously considering winter hibernation in this frigid weather.

"I'm saying don't get banished from the city before they've realized your true potential. And seriously, quit biting your lower lip."

I liberate my teeth from my chapped lip. "You know me far too well. I wish you were here with us."

"You're going to be fantastic. And remember, I'm just a phone call away."

"I located it - Arctic Ice Rink," I read the sign on the two story building.

"Good, you'll know exactly where you need to be tomorrow."

I sigh, "I'm nervous. This job means a lot to me. I really hope it pans out."

"Cut the self-doubt. You got this. You're going to be the best Social Media Manager in all of Montana. Plus, think about the hunky hockey players you'll be meeting. They'll be swooning all over the sexy, copper haired newcomer in town."

"No puck bunny aspirations here. I've got too much invested in this job to skate around on thin ice with romance. Plus, my heart's RSVP'd 'no more drama,' in this century."

"I get how crucial this job is for you, but don't forget to carve out some 'me time'. You've been neglecting that for the past several years."

"I love the game of hockey, and now it's my job to promote it."

"Just a heads-up, you know there's always that one hotshot player itching to ruffle feathers. Don't let him."

"I filed that in my mental playbook. This job is just a stepping stone. Nail it in the ECHL, the NHL will be knocking at my door - that's the dream."

"Did you get settled into the rental house?"

"Yeah, it's snug, but it's our budget friendly home for now. I'm just grateful it comes with heat." I tug my jacket closer. "My hands are on the verge of frostbite. I'm going to hang up and hit the cute little cafe across the street."

"Give Koti a kiss for me."

"I will. She already misses you. I'll call you after my meeting tomorrow."

"Break a leg, but let's keep it figuratively," she chuckles.

"Thanks, Maggs."

Maggie Sheldon and I go way back - friends since our freshman year of high school. Her parent's split, and her mom whisked her away from New York City to Harmony Grove. Initially, she detested the place and struggled to fit in until she crossed paths with me. Our connection? A shared love for reading, despite our divergent tastes. She was into Dystopia fiction, while I swooned over all things romance, especially small-town love stories. No matter the plot, they always cumulated in a couple finding their way to love, and their predictability was my solace. I was a firm believer in true love...until I wasn't. That's a topic I consciously avoid delving into. I remind myself: no love, no heartbreak - I've already had my fill.

Darting across the street, I can't help but wish I had traded these fashion-forward boots for a pair of ice skates. My attempt at a winter sprint turns into a stumbling spectacle, and just before I become a real life snow angel, I'm saved by a hand catching me. While it prevented a complete ice-induced catastrophe, I still find myself in an unplanned sitting position - not exactly a graceful one. More like a goose trying to do an impromptu split. It's not a coordinated scene from one of my figure skating competitions, more like a quirky version of yours truly and an unintentional goose interpretation fully equipped with a similar sound leaving my mouth.

"Whoa," a man's voice rings out.

I glance up, and bam! There stands a man who could give Adonis a run for his money - we're talking god-like gorgeous. His soft hazel eyes are like two warm campfires, instantly thawing my frozen heart, or at least my frost-bitten fingers.

"You really should watch your step," he says, helping me up. "Perhaps a new pair of boots wouldn't hurt," he adds, speaking without smiling, as if passing judgment on my poor choice of footwear.

I start to thank him, but he dashes into the cafe, leaving me with the door closing in my face. "Not exactly a knight in shining armor," I grumble, shaking off the snowy aftermath.

The aroma inside the cafe is heavenly. Scattered small tables and a line of people at the counter create an inviting atmosphere. I tap the shoulder of the guy that prevented my head from meeting the ice covered pavement. He turns, zeroing in on me with intensity.

"I just wanted to say thank you." As he continues to stare, I can't help but turn my gratitude into a full-blown appreciation of his appearance. Tall, a solid 6'2", with wheat-colored hair peeking out under his beanie. And that neatly kept goatee and mustache in a darker shade of brown, just complete the drool-worthy masterpiece of this guy.

I ditch my glove and offer my hand. "Piper," I introduce myself.

One corner of his mouth turns upward into a smile - well, at least I think it's an attempt at one. "Jake," he grunts.

"I'm new in town." I plaster on a warm grin.

"Good for you," he replies, about as friendly as a cactus.

"So, not a fan of newcomers," I say, my smile slipping.

He leans in with all the friendliness of a bear with a sore paw, asks, "What do you want from me? An autograph? A picture? Perhaps a date? A night in my bed?"

"I...um," stammer, caught completely off guard.

"I'm so done with puck bunnies. Just, please, leave me alone," he pivots, turning his back to me and yanking off his beanie. A cascade of wheat-colored curls spills down to his mid-shoulders.

Ah, the legendary *Hockey-flow*. This must be the cocky player Maggs warned me about. I should probably take her advice and let it slide - *seriously, Piper, let it go*. But nope, I can't resist.

"Are you always this charming to strangers? Ever think that I might just be trying to say thank you?" I retort, giving him my best scowl.

He whirls around. "No, it didn't. Because every woman in this town wants something from me!" His words echo loudly even though he's saying them just loud enough for me to hear.

"Even if you were the only man in this town, I wouldn't swap a puck for your autograph, a slap-shot selfie, a date (guaranteed penalty minutes), or a hat trick in your bed," I declare with such volume heads turn in our direction. It's like I just dropped a mic in the middle of the chilly town square. Or maybe my version of a power play.

The patrons exhibit a mix of reactions - a sprinkle of gasps from the ladies and a hearty applause from the men.

"I knew it. You're nothing but a puck bunny tossing around hockey terms, hoping to impress me," he scoffs.

I don't care if he's Adonis's long-lost twin; he's a human heater making the chill do the cha-cha out of my body, and not in a way that makes a woman feel good. "So, you're saying a gal can't know her hockey without it being a secret plan to hit on you? Classic."

"You're just mad because I'm not trying to get under your skirt," he rambles.

"First of all, it's colder than a polar bear's fridge. I'm not rocking a skirt, and even if I were, I'd have tied it around my knees - a preemptive move to keep your hands off the ice!"

He grins. "What's second on the list?"

Did I have a second point? His smile is like a magic trick, distracting me. Those teeth must be

Hollywood level veneers; hockey players are usually part-time tooth fairy donors. I mentally roll my eyes to regain focus. "Secondly, congratulations! You've officially earned the title of Class-A-Ass!."

"Wow! Where did you say you were from, Poppy?" His eyes light up.

"It's Piper! And, I didn't!" I spin on my winter-gear-challenged boots, executing a not too graceful move, swinging the door open, stepping onto the snow-covered sidewalk. I cinch my scarf together like it's the latest runway accessory and march toward the outdoor clothing store on the corner.

"A night in my bed," I'm still mumbling in a mocking tone when I enter the store. A bell jingles announcing my entrance.

"Welcome to Seth's Outdoor Store," a man that appears to be in his late fifties greets me.

"I'm relieved someone's rolling out the welcoming mat in this town," I say underneath my breath. "Are you Seth?"

He emerges from the counter, hand extended. "Seth Spencer. And who might you be? I know just about everyone in this town, and I've never laid eyes on your pretty face before."

"I just moved here from North Carolina," I shake his hand.

"That's a beautiful state. What brings you to Montana?"

"A job."

"Well, I hope you find it more exciting than the winter weather," he chuckles, sliding his hands into his pockets. "Is there something I can help you find?"

I glance down at my feet. "I need boots that will prevent me from pulling another accidental pirouette in the middle of the icy street, other than ice skates," I laugh.

"I've got just the pair for you. Follow me."

"This is a charming store."

"Thanks. It's been in my family for two generations."

"Do you have an online storefront?"

"Regrettably, that's a bit beyond my skill set. If my son were interested in taking over, he'd probably manage it."

"Sounds like he's not keen on the family business."

"The hockey bug bit him hard and won't let him go," he chuckles.

"I could set up an online store if you'd like?"

He stops at a stack of boxes. "What size do you wear?"

"Eight."

He scans the boxes until he finds the right size. "That's mighty kind of you to offer, but I'm getting to the point where I'd rather retire than take on new challenges."

As I perch on the bench, wrestling off my soggy boots, he eyeballs my pitiful situation.

"Looks like your feet are on a cold, wet adventure, too. Let me snag you a pair of socks," he offers.

This place triggers a wave of nostalgia, a pleasant flashback to the General Market, where I worked on weekends back in my hometown. It's like a warm, inviting hug in this frozen frontier.

"Here you go," he hands me a pair of wool knee-high socks. "Even if you don't buy the boots, those are on the house."

I roll them up and shoehorn my foot into the sheepskin-lined, waterproof boots with soles that could probably withstand a snowstorm apocalypse. "These are perfect. Do you have any in pint-sized versions for kiddos?"

"I've got just the thing. How old is your little one?"

"She's four," I reply, deciding to skip the correction - the backstory is too painful.

"I've got the perfect pink pair for a four-year-old princess." He proudly presents them to me.

They are both more expensive than I planned on paying, but I'll have a steady paycheck soon to afford them. I follow him to the counter and take out my credit card.

"Oh, I forgot to tell you. On Monday's everything is half-off."

I glance around the store looking for signs screaming half off Mondays. *Don't point it out, just say thank you, Piper.* "That's great. Thank you. I'll be sure to come back and purchase a heavier jacket."

He plunges his hand into a wooden barrel of assorted candies by the front door. "And here, a little treat for you kiddo," he slips it into my bag.

"Thanks a bunch," I chirp.

Uncertain if it's possible, but the ice seems thicker in the short time I was in the store. I'm thankful for my new boots keeping me upright when I cross the street. I see Jake leaving the cafe with his beanie back in action. Swiftly averting my eyes to avoid another encounter with him, I'm grateful not everyone in this town is as brash as he is. Maybe a crash course in manners from the outdoor store owner would do him some good.

2 PIPER

"What's wrong, dear?" my mother calls out from the quaint teal-covered porch.

"My car won't start," I exclaim as I slam the door. "I think the battery doesn't like this cold weather any more than I do."

"Come inside and thaw out."

"I can't. I'm already going to be late for my first meeting."

"At least come inside until you figure out how you're going to get to work."

I stomp the snow off my boots on the doormat. "I'll have to call an Uber." Browsing through the app, I continue into the kitchen to pour a cup of coffee.

"Can I go outside and build a snowman?" Koti tugs on her new boots.

"Not right now, sweetie. I have to get to work."

"Grandma can take me," she pouts.

"How about we eat some breakfast first," my mom suggests, placing a plate of pancakes on the four-person round table.

I glance at my watch. "The Uber driver will be here in ten minutes. That will make me thirty minutes late."

"Here, eat a pancake," Mom insists.

"To be honest, I'm too nervous to eat. The thought of getting fired on my first day is making me queasy. I've relocated us halfway around the country for this job. I adore Harmony Grove, but the prospect of going back and admitting failure is daunting."

"I'm sure you aren't the first person to be late because of car issues. It must happen all the time out here," my mom reassures, the eternal optimist.

"Mommy, stay home and build a snowman with me, please." Her blue-green eyes, a mirror of her father's, twinkle with excitement.

"I wish I could. I promise we'll build one when I get back." I thumb a lock of her golden-hair behind her ear.

My phone pings. "My Uber is here. Gotta run." I plant a kiss on Koti's freckled nose and dash out.

The snow falls heavily, delaying the drive to the ice rink. I arrive forty-five minutes late for my meeting. I long for warmth, but when I open the door, I'm greeted by arctic air.

"I have a meeting with Mr.Robinson," I inform the person at the front desk.

"Second level, third door on the right," he guides me.

I ascend the stairs and find the door with the prestigious nameplate - Charlie Robinson, Arctic Wolves Team Manager. Unwinding my scarf and shoving it into my bag, I attempt to tame my hair. Right as I'm about to knock, the door swings open, and I'm met with light hazel eyes rimmed with brown, freezing me in place.

"You," he smirks. "Are you stalking me now?"

I frown, mentally wishing my boots had GPS to navigate straight to his...personal hockey stick. "No. I have a meeting with Mr. Robinson."

He swings the door wide, and there sits the team manager behind a large oak desk in a sharp looking business suit. "This is who you've been waiting for?" Jake's voice rises.

Peering over his silver-framed glasses, Mr. Robinson says, "Yes, please come in."

"You're late," Jake interjects, his tone testy.

I scowl and push past him. "I'm so sorry Mr. Robinson..."

"Call me Charlie, please," he stands like a true gentleman.

"Charlie," I say, shedding my coat and feeling like the sun just burst into this office. "My car decided to pull a Monday morning and refused to start."

"A lame excuse," Jake mutters next to my ear.

I stick out my palm as Charlie approaches.

"I'm thrilled to have you on board," his smile is sincere.

"Wait, you are working for the Arctic Wolves?" Jake scowls, or perhaps that's just his permanent facial setting when he's around me.

"I take it you two have met," Charlie chuckles.

"If you call saving her ass from being plastered on the ice and then giving me a not-so-subtle stare-down at the cafe as rudeness, then yes," Jake crosses his arms over his chest.

"I wasn't gawking at you. Your ego has no bounds," I declare, determined not to be swayed by his charming looks and laid-back vibe. His choice of dark-denim paired with a short-sleeved team shirt that flaunts his lean, muscular arms, *with a tattoo I vow to pretend doesn't exist,* is very disarming.

Undeterred, I extend my hand toward him, ready to hit the reset button. "We haven't officially met. I'm Piper Malone. The team's new Social Media Manager."

He eyes my outstretched hand as if it's a dangerous creature with eye-scratching capabilities, *not that the thought hasn't crossed my mind.* After a dramatic huff that could win awards, he finally surrenders his palm to the potential menace in mine.

I find myself daydreaming about flooding the social media page with cringe-worthy photos of him, but reality taps me on the shoulder and reminds me unemployment is not on my bucket list. Is there anything more exhausting than a man who thinks he's above social pleasantries, all because he won the genetic lottery in looks and talent? He's burned through my tolerance of self-important asshats. Still, I have to play nice.

"Again, I apologize for being late." I take out my laptop, draping my bag over the chair, and take the seat across from Charlie. "I have a plethora of ideas for the team and individual player showcases."

"Before you go any further," Charlie raises his hand. "I've already seen your talent. I trust you with whatever plan you've come up with for the team." He rests back in his chair, folding his hands on his desk. "I fully expect every player to cooperate," he shoots a pointed look at Jake, who huffs for the second time, but doesn't argue with him.

"As you've already experienced, our star player, Spencer, while dazzling on the ice, is a bit of a handful. He could use a new look on our platforms. He will be your biggest challenge," he laughs.

"I doubt she can handle it," Jake snarls.

My jaw drops, not sure what to say to that. Maggs voice echoes in my head, warning me again about the hotshot player with a penchant for feather-ruffling. *Jake Spencer fills these shoes, or should I say ice skates.*

Charlie chuckles, seemingly enjoying the drama. "I'm sure you've handled your share of egotistical athletes. I've read about your promising figure-skating past for the US Olympics. If I may ask, what happened?"

Life, a tragedy, an unexpected child to raise are the true answers, but I opt for a simpler, less compli- cated one. "An injury."

"I'm so sorry to hear that. It's difficult to lose something you've dedicated your life to," he looks genuinely empathetic.

"I'm sure in your line of work, you've seen it plenty," I deflect. "I've had time to recalibrate my focus on something else that I love. That's what brings me here."

Charlie hands me a folder. "This is the team's schedule. Work your magic around it. Emails and phone numbers of the players are in there too. Feel free to schedule them with you when they are not required to be on the ice. And, let me know if any of them give you an issue."

Jake shoots me a look that could melt glaciers, sending a prickling sensation down my spine. "I get to approve every picture of me before it's posted."

An irritable laugh lurches from me. "According to my contract, I have the final say."

He narrows his gaze at Charlie. "Really?"

Charlie backs me up with a nod. "Indeed."

"But," I say, standing up, "I'll take your opinion into consideration." *Liar*, my brain says. I'll be posting what will gain the most views.

Charlie checks his watch. "Anything else you need from me? I've got a meeting waiting for me."

"This will suffice," I say, giving the folder a casual wave before stashing it, along with my laptop, into my bag. "I'll have some photos on your desk by the end of the week."

Charlie adds one more thing to the mix, opening a filing cabinet. "And you'll need these credentials for the games."

"Thank you."

As I make my exit, to my surprise, or slight unnerving, Jake decides to join me on the descent down the stairs. We're not exactly thrilled to collaborate, but a truce is in order.

"Would you like to schedule your appointment with me since we're face to face?" I inquire politely.

He throws me a curious glance. "You never told me where you were from?"

"North Carolina."

"Here in Montana, we aren't easily charmed by pretty redheads, so don't go thinking you'll be attaching yourself to any of my teammates. Keep it professional," he warns, before striding off into a locker room.

Well, scratch the peace treaty idea. *He thinks*

I'm pretty. If he wouldn't have bolted off so quickly, I would have been in his face telling him that this redhead is about as attracted to him as a cat to a bath.

I whip out my phone, GPS-ing a bookstore a few blocks south of the ice rink. Despite the scarf half-covering my face, snowflakes decide to play peek-aboo with my lashes. Carefully navigating the icy sidewalks, I safely arrive, with zero goose looking mishaps, at the entrance of the bookstore. Warmth hits me as I step inside, greeted by a crackling fire-place and soft overhead music. A handful of people mill about. I spot a comfy two person table near the fireplace and stake claim before delving into my scheduling endeavors. But first, a call to Maggs.

"How'd your debut meeting go?" she inquires without a hello.

"I was late, but the team manager was a gem. He's already seen my work and showered me with everything I need.

"Efficient," she remarks. "So, why is there a hint of annoyance in your voice?"

"Remember the hotshot player you warned me about? He graced the meeting. Worst of all, we randomly crossed paths yesterday, and now he has a grudge against me."

"How could anyone not like you?" she laughs. "Is he, like, hot?"

I blink rapidly. "Drop-dead gorgeous, but an asshat."

"Then your strategy is clear - keep a safe distance from him. If he gets out of line, just say the word and I'll come help you bury his body."

Her dark humor always manages to draw a smile from me. "I don't think it would bode well for my career if I took out their star player."

"True, true. I'm sure you'll win him over in no time."

"All I want to do is excel at my job, climb the ladder to the big leagues, and earn enough money to settle all the overdue bills while taking care of Mom and Koti."

"You do have the insurance money your sister left you," she suggests.

"I want to reserve that for Koti's future."

"You could borrow from it temporarily and pay it back later when you're rolling in cash."

"I'm determined to make it on my own."

"Raising Koti wasn't supposed to be on your agenda. Haven't you sacrificed enough? You were destined for a spot on the Olympics in figure skating, and you turned it down."

"I had to, Maggs. My mom couldn't handle Koti alone."

"You're unbelievably self-sacrificing. I doubt I could have done the same thing in your shoes."

"There wasn't a choice and I'm making the best of it."

"You know I've got your back."

"Come for a visit as soon as you can get away. I miss you."

"I will, I promise."

I dedicate the next few hours to coffee sipping and Arctic Wolves player profiling.

Jake Spencer, last year's forward sensation, seems to have misplaced his scoring mojo this season. I play detective searching for clues - injuries, traumatic events, or perhaps an encounter with a rogue Zamboni. Instead, I'm bombarded with pictures of Jake and different women on his arm in the local paper. He's the lone Summit Ridge ambassador on the team.

"He's a local celeb," I chuckle to myself, digging deeper. Then it hits me like a hockey puck in the face. "No way!" A front-page news article unveils the father-son duo: Seth Spencer is Jake's dad. Apparently, the charm gene took a detour around the family tree. They're about as alike as a goalie and a ballerina.

3 PIPER

"Mommy!" Koti giggles the moment I open the door. "You gotta see the snowman me and Meme made. It's got a carrot nose, just like Frosty the Snowman. But we couldn't find a hat so we gave it a snowman hairdo," she says, making a cute little pout and tugging at my hand, urging me to come see. "It was so much fun, Mommy!"

"Sounds like you and Meme had a fun day."

She drags me through the kitchen where I find Mom sipping on a mug of hot chocolate, looking a bit tired, flipping through a stack of mail. "How did your first day on the job go?"

"I'll tell you all about it, but first, I have to see the snowman Koti is super excited to show me."

Koti wrestles her tiny feet into her boots and yanks a super bright pink beanie over her ears before zipping out the back door. "Look," she exclaims, pointing dramatically. "Isn't he huge!"

In reality, the snowman measures a whopping two feet, but in her world, he's ginormous. "You and Meme did an amazing job. I totally love the pasta noodles you used for hair."

"Meme helped me turn them blue."

"That explains the stylish blue beard on your chin," I tease, letting out a chuckle.

"I got hungry," she says, lifting a shoulder in defense.

"You did an awesome job, sweetie. Stand next to him and I'll take your picture. Aunt Maggs will go crazy for it."

She scurries to the snowman's side, plants a hand on her hip, and tilts her head with a four-year-old attitude. "Cheese," she squeals, and I quickly snap the picture with my phone.

"How about you go inside and get cleaned up for dinner?"

"Can I pretty please have hot chocolate with lots of marshmallows?"

"Before bedtime, I promise."

"Okay," she mumbles, a bit disappointed.

Once indoors, she kicks off her boots and skips to the bathroom to wash her little hands.

I shed my coat, boots, and sock hat. "Seeing that pile of mail, I'm guessing our bills decided to tag along to Montana."

"It's funny how they do that," my mom laughs halfheartedly.

"I don't want you to worry about them. I'm going to take care of it."

"But there are so many, and they just keep piling up with interest. You'll never get above water."

"I'll try negotiating with them for the umpteenth time. I've got a good job now, making a lot more money." Even with that, I know we'll still be barely keeping afloat. My contract with the Arctic Wolves prevents me from taking on other social media jobs. Maybe I can barter an online presence with Seth in exchange for part-time employment.

"I could look into finding a job in the evenings and on weekends," she offers.

"No. You are already juggling a lot with Koti, and I won't have you working late. You're tired enough when I get home."

"What if we enrolled Koti in pre-school? Then I could work during the day to help out."

"You know that was never in the plan for Koti to attend any kind of public school system. Liv and James didn't want that for their daughter."

"Dying wasn't part of their design," she sniffs, her eyes filling up with tears.

Strolling around the table, I envelop her in my arms, resting my chin on her shoulder. "I miss them too. We're both doing the best we can given the circumstances. It will all be okay. I promise." I don't know how, but it has to be. We were left with no choice.

Emma Malone has never had an easy life. She single-handedly raised Liv and me. Our father, her husband, went out one night for a pack of cigarettes when I was only a year old, and never returned. Our mother worked tirelessly at a diner, bringing home food for us, often skipping her own meals to ensure we had enough to eat. She made sure we had everything we needed, never sparing a thought for herself. Liv and I had a pact that once we were grown, we'd take care of her, and she'd never have to worry about working again. Plans are great until life throws you a curve ball.

"I'm ready for hot chocolate," Koti exclaims, rubbing her hands together.

"Meme made something that smells delicious," I say.

"It's a pot of chicken noodle soup. Just overlook the blue tint," she says, standing and grinning. Little miss got carried away and dyed all the noodles before I could snag some for the soup."

"Oops, sorry, Meme," Koti scrunches her nose.

"It's alright. It will eat the same, and who knows, it might become a famous recipe," she tweaks Koti's cheek.

"I'll snap some photos and post them on my Instagram site. My followers with kiddos will eat it up."

Mom ladles soup into bowls and slices a loaf of warm sourdough bread, generously spreading butter on a piece before putting it on Koti's plate. We gather around the table, saying the blessing before eagerly diving in.

"So, how was your first day?" Mom inquires again.

"It went well. I've already mapped out the week and reached out to a few of the players for a photo shoot. They've got practice tomorrow, so I'll snag some candid shots."

"Any handsome hockey players catch your eye?" Mom teases.

"I did meet one that's a bit full of himself, but I'm here for work, not to find a date. Strictly business," I emphasize.

"You haven't been on a date since you and David broke up," Mom remarks, slurping from her spoon.

"Who is David?" Koti asks, a noodle clinging to her chin.

"A jerk," I sputter before thinking.

"You said a bad word," Koti scowls.

"I'm sorry, you're right. He's someone who doesn't matter to any of us," I quickly correct.

"He was your mommy's boyfriend before you came along," Mom spills the beans.

"Mom!" I shoot her a disapproving look.

"Did you love him?" Koti asks without missing a beat.

"That's a big talk to have with a four-year-old. Just eat your soup," I tap my spoon on the side of the bowl.

"I'm all done. Can I have hot chocolate now?" Koti beams, showing off her blue tinged teeth.

"I'll get it," Mom volunteers, getting to her feet.

"Don't forget the marshmallows," Koti adds.

"Is there a 'please' in there somewhere?" Mom asks, glancing back.

"Please, Meme."

"After you're done with your cocoa, I'll tuck you into bed."

"Will you tell me the story of Princess Olivia and Prince James?"

"Yes," I agree, even though it breaks my heart every time I tell her.

After dinner, I tackle the dishes and head to Koti's room. Her space fits only a twin bed and a three-drawer dresser. She's decked out in pink long johns, snug under her ice hockey-themed comforter. She probably knows more about the game of hockey than most adults.

"Are you going to take me to a game?" she asks.

"I will, but not this week. Mommy needs to settle into her new job first."

"Okay," she says, lifting the comforter for me to curl in next to her.

She snuggles on her side underneath my arm, and I run my fingers through her golden-colored hair.

"Once upon a time, there was a princess named Olivia. She lived in a castle in the forest."

"She was a princess over the animals," Koti corrects.

"Who is telling the story, you or me?" I laugh and continue. "A princess over all of the animals in the forest. Animals of all types flocked to her. Her best friend was a black panther named Panda."

"That's a silly name for a panther," she remarks with a big yawn.

"One day, a handsome prince wandered into the forest searching for his horse. Panda pounced on him and dragged him to Princess Olivia."

"She fell in love with him and made him a prince," Koti's eyes flutter close.

"James declared his love for her but had to prove to Panda that he wasn't going to harm any of them. James, with kindness and sincerity, earned Panda's trust by helping the animals in the forest. Princess Olivia and Prince James, bound by love, ruled the enchanted kingdom hand in hand. They shared their castle with the creatures of the woods, creating a happy place for all of them. Despite Princess Olivia's immense love for all the animals, she yearned for a baby of her own."

Soft snores emanate from Koti, who without fail, falls asleep before the end of the story. It's a good thing since I haven't quite devised the fairy-tale where their happily ever after unfolds without their baby girl.

Mom pokes her head in the door. "Is she sleeping?"

I nod, easing myself from the bed, tiptoeing out of the room.

"Are you ever going to finish the story?" she lovingly rubs my shoulder.

"I'm hoping she grows out of fairy-tales before I have to."

"We'll have to tell her one day."

"I know, but for now, I just want her to be a happy, normal kid."

"Liv would be so proud of you."

"Thanks, Mom."

She retreats to her bedroom and I escape into a long, hot shower. Glancing over the file one more time before calling it a night, confirming the practice time in the morning.

AT THE CRACK OF DAWN, I step into the ice rink, shuffling my way inside. Charlie beckons me over as soon as he spots me. Dressed in sweats, he's just as handsome as when he's in a polished suit. "Wolves, I want you to officially meet our new Social Media Manager. This is Ms. Piper Malone. I expect you to cooperate fully with her on your off times.

He introduces the players, going through the first line one by one - "Justin, Brady, Bohdi, Remi, Karter, and you've already met Jake, who grunts in my direction. Moving on to the second and third lines, some greet me with handshakes, while others offer nods.

"It's very nice to meet all of you. I've already spoken with a few of you and have set dates and times for photos and interviews. I'll stick around after practice if you'd like to schedule your time with me."

I climb the concrete bleacher to watch the players in action. This year's rookies, Remi and Karter, seemed to have blended seamlessly. They glide effortlessly over the ice, and Jake stands out as one of the fastest skaters I've witnessed, as if he was born on blades instead of feet. The line sets up their play, passing the puck to Jake, who misses the goal. He swears loudly, and they try again with the same outcome.

"Get your head together!" Charlie yells, waving him off the ice.

Having watched replays of their games from last year, where Jake rarely missed a shot, I notice he skates with the same intensity but hesitates a solid second before swinging his stick. I wonder if he realizes he's doing it. Something is clearly holding him back.

I weave my way around the perimeter of the

rink, snapping photos, catching some really great shots.

"I heard we had a new woman on board," a lady with long blonde hair slicked back in a ponytail, donning a team jersey, says next to me. "I'm Hensley, the team physician." Her smile is warm and welcoming.

"Piper," I respond, shaking her hand. "It's so nice to meet you."

"Likewise. It's wonderful to have another female working for the Arctic Wolves."

"Are there any injured players on the team currently? I'd love to interview them with you."

"Fortunately, not at this time, we don't. But you know how quickly that can change. I read your file. You had a promising future in figure skating. I heard you were injured."

"Yeah, I broke my hip on a hard fall." It's the lie I've told everyone.

Her brow furrows. "At your age, it should have healed well enough for you to return to the ice. I could help you if you'd like."

"Thanks, but I've moved on. I love this just as much as figure skating. Plus, I get to help other athletes achieve their dreams through exposure."

As Jake skates back onto the ice, I inquire, all while snapping photos. "Has 24 had any recent injuries?"

"He had a minor one mid-season last year, but he didn't let it slow him down. Why do you ask?"

"Just curious about what might have changed. His scoring is off."

"It probably has more to do with his head being on the ladies rather than the game. His bedroom has been like a glass revolving door," she huffs. "Someone needs to get him to refocus and stay away from the women. It's not all his fault; women throw themselves at his feet. Young, hot, gorgeous jock." She fishes a business card from her jacket pocket. "Give me a call, and we'll meet."

"Thanks," I respond, as she turns and walks away. "Poor Jake, too good-looking, a plethora of women, and broken hearts in his wake," I snark to myself.

4 JAKE

"What the hell is eating you, bro?" Bohdi whips off his helmet. "You're playing like shit."

"I know, man. I'm distracted."

"Being all caught up in the romance department is your issue. How many hours of sleep are you getting a night?"

"Not many."

"You're jeopardizing your shot at the NHL, for what? Getting laid?"

"I'm an idiot."

"You need to keep it in your pants and focus on the game."

"Women are constantly throwing themselves at me, and I lack self-control."

"We should find you a fake girlfriend to ward off other women, one who isn't interested in having sex with you."

"In this town, that's not possible." Movement at the edge of the ice grabs my attention. Dr. Hensley is talking to the new Social Media Manager. "Wait, I might just have the perfect solution."

His gaze follows mine. "Dr. Hensley? You're out of your mind," Bohdi slaps me on the back.

"Not her. Piper."

"She works for the team. You can't mess around with her."

"She can't stand me."

"Yeah, but look at her man, she's gorgeous. I'd love to run my fingers through that red hair of hers."

"You missed the point. She despises me," I pronounce each word slowly. "She wouldn't let me near her."

"Why do you think she doesn't like you?"

"I was an intentional dick to her, because I thought she wanted to get in my pants like every other woman in this town."

"It's not like you've made yourself unavailable to any of them," he chuckles.

"If I don't get my head back in the game, I might as well go work with my father."

"Your dad's a good man."

"Regardless, I don't want the family business. All I've ever wanted to do is play hockey, and I'm this close to moving up," I pinch my fingers together. "Coach said that if I performed as well as last season, I'd be playing in the NHL by the end of the year."

He stands. "Then I suggest you get down on your knees and plead with the woman that dislikes you so much to be your pretend girlfriend. Good luck with that," he snorts. "And don't forget to bring a suitcase full of cash; you're going to need it," he adds before putting on his helmet, skating out onto the ice.

Coach summons me to return to the ice, but within minutes, I'm shown the exit for checking my own teammate too hard. "You're done for the day! Get off the ice, and I'll see you in my office at noon. Don't make me wait," he warns.

Tossing my helmet aside, I lean my stick against the wall and run my hands through the damp strands of my hair that have fallen loose. Biting the inside of my cheek, I decide to track down Piper. She's moved to the bleachers, absorbed in scrolling through her camera.

"Hey," I nonchalantly greet her, meeting her on the top bleacher.

"Did you finally decide to schedule an appointment with me?" she asks, bitterness evident in her tone.

"I think we got off on the wrong foot."

"You think?" she retorts.

I settle on the concrete next to her. "Is there something you need?" *This isn't coming out right. How do you ask a woman you don't even know to be your fake girlfriend?*

"All I need from you is to schedule a time to have a few photos taken off the ice."

"That's not what I mean." I adjust to face her. "Like, is there something personal you need?"

"A quarter of a million dollars would do," she laughs. "What kind of question is that?"

"Done. I'll write you a check."

Her mouth drops open, then there's a dangerous look brewing in her grey eyes. One that says my balls are in great danger. *Damn, her eyes are rimmed in green; I didn't notice how unique they were before.*

"I don't know what kind of woman you think I am, but my body is not for sale," she stands, and I grab her hand.

Her words in the cafe flash through my mind. *"I'm not rocking a skirt, and even if I were, I'd have tied it around my knees - a preemptive move to keep your hands off the ice!"*

"I don't want your ice...I mean body." Actually, she's pretty damn hot. I'd say five seven, slender, not too curvy, and that copper hair is a turn on. I'd like to trail my tongue over the freckles scattered over the bridge of her nose. *Focus, Jake, focus.*

"Good, because you'd be the last guy in this town I'd let touch me."

"You've made that perfectly clear not once but twice." My ego should be taking a hit. "That's why I need your help. You hate me."

"You're really strange Jake, and offensive."

"I know. None of this is coming out like I planned."

She jerks her hand free of mine. "Why are you offering me money?" She crosses her arms over her chest.

"I'm in a bit of a slump. Women throw themselves at me on a daily basis."

"I'm not one of them," she snips.

"Exactly. I can't focus on the game because I'm exhausted all the time and I'm constantly breaking their hearts because I can't commit."

"Poor Jake," she mock pouts.

"Look, we can help each other out. I need a fake girlfriend so women will leave me alone. One that doesn't want to sleep with me."

"Well, that surely wouldn't be a problem," she grunts.

"You said you needed money. If you'll agree to be my girlfriend in public, at the end of the season, I'll give you the cash."

She gnaws at the inside of her cheek like she's considering it. "I'd rather be broke," she storms off.

"If you change your mind, you have my number," I yell. Damn, I've never had such a gorgeous woman so put off by me. It's kinda hot.

After a quick shower, I head to Charlie's office. He glances at his watch, interrupting his phone conversation when I walk in. "Two minutes early," I say, taking a seat across from his desk.

He hangs up the phone. "I don't know what's going on with you, but you damn sure better figure it out, or you're going to lose your chance to play any higher. In fact, I should trade you down."

"I'm going to fix it, sir." I fidget in my chair.

He rocks back with his hands clasped behind his head. "I'm dead serious. We have a game on our ice next week and if your head isn't in the game, I'll bench you."

"It will be, I promise."

"Get your blades on and meet with the shooting coach."

"Yes, sir." I stand to walk out, and his secretary walks into the office.

"Hi, Jake," she winks and slyly runs her hand over my ass.

"I gotta go," I growl and huff out. "No more sex," I chant under my breath. Not until I'm back in the game.

Deep within, I recognize that my perceived lack of self-control with women isn't the true obstacle holding me back. It's merely a convenient explanation and an excuse. In reality, my sex life isn't as active as my teammates believe, at least not like it was in the beginning. Nowadays, it's sporadic due to the fact I'm finding it a turnoff that women in this town really do throw themselves at me, and, well, being a guy, I sometimes find it hard to resist. Despite being upfront about it only being a casual relationship, they don't really hear me. I'm not looking to commit to anything other than the game of hockey. Creating a fictional girlfriend could divert them and afford me time to grapple with my own guilt. However, she despises me to the extent she turned down a quarter of a million dollars.

After concluding my session with the shooting coach, I walk down the snow-filled sidewalks to the sporting goods store, a local staple where people hold my father in high regard. Seth Spencer is a good, hardworking, and devoted family man. He's endured a lot of pain in his life, but he's never let it affect him. After ten years of marriage to the woman that owned his heart, she abandoned him and us when my baby sister, Jewels, was born. She couldn't cope with the fact that Jewels was deaf, leaving my dad to raise us. I was only five at the time, but I've never forgotten her betrayal and the nasty divorce that followed. As a teenager, I vowed never to marry, because I saw the pain etched in my father's face whenever her name was mentioned.

"Hey, Pops," I say as I step into the store.

"I'm surprised you came by," he responds, embracing me.

"I promised I'd help you with the inventory," I mention, shrugging out of my coat.

"Jewels and I took care of it yesterday, so you're off the hook."

"I'm sorry. Is there anything else I can do to help you?"

"You're a busy man, son. I get that hockey is your priority."

He doesn't say it to make me feel guilty, but I can't help it. He's been nothing but supportive of me. I believe he always knew I wouldn't take over the business. He could sell this place and retire comfortably, but he chooses not to. Jewels stepped up and decided to learn the business, and she's great at it. This community adores her, and so do I.

A tap on my shoulder prompts me to turn around. Jewels signs, "I've missed you. You haven't been around much."

"I know, I'm sorry," I sign back. "I have a game next week and tickets waiting for the two of you." She can read lips, but I always communicate with my hands.

"You're going to go so far this year," her hands move rapidly before she hugs me.

She and Dad have consistently been my most enthusiastic supporters, sharing a deep love for the game. Jewels used to follow me on the ice. I taught her how to skate and she's so graceful. She wanted to be a figure skater, but she couldn't feel the music and gave up. Trying her hand at hockey, her petite stature made it too physically demanding.

"How about I treat you both to a late dinner?"

"I'd like that. It's been a while since the three of us shared a meal. I'll flip the closed sign around on the door," Pops moves past me to lock up.

"How are your business classes going?" I inquire of Jewels.

"Great. It's my last class," she beams, making a joyful sign with her hands.

At twenty-one, Jewels is set to graduate at the end of the semester with her master's degree in business. Always the academic achiever, she excels at her studies.

"How does a good greasy burger sound?" our father asks, laying his hand on my shoulder.

Jewels claps her hands.

"Alright, a burger it is."

We all put our coats on and brave the wind and snow to the mom-and-pop restaurant two blocks down, known for serving the best burgers, French fries, and chocolate milkshakes in town.

The hostess greets me with a grin and a wink, eyeing me like I'm a piece of meat. I press my lips together and shove my hands in my pockets.

My father steps up and requests a booth.

"Follow me," she says with extra flair to her hips, licking her red lips.

I take a seat in the booth beside Jewels, and Pops sits across from us as he thanks the hostess.

"It was my pleasure," she purrs, sinking her fingernails into my shoulder before she walks away.

"Quite the ladies' man," my sister signs, laughing.

5 PIPER

"It sounds like you had a productive day," Maggs says, patiently enduring my thirty minute excited ramble.

"Productivity was my middle name today. I captured some amazing shots of the players. They've all been cooperative..."

"Except for Mr. Adonis, I presume," she interrupts with a snort.

"Yeah, that guy. Wait till you hear what he offered me."

"Spill it," she urges, clearly amused.

"He tried to bribe me a fat quarter of a million dollars to be his pretend girlfriend for the hockey season."

"Please tell me you took him up on it," her voice hits a high note.

"Come on, Maggs! With his reputation, that offer is sketchier than a cat on a hot tin roof," I retort.

"A quarter of a million could wipe your problems away, Piper. What's the harm? You'd keep him in check."

"It just feels...I don't know, a bit like a bargain bin romance."

"I'd wear cheap proudly if it meant shedding the mountain of bills I'm buried under. Seriously, reconsider and slap some ground rules on that hot mess."

"I can't imagine it's a stellar career move to entertain the idea of dating one of the players."

"Will your career ever pay off your stack of bills? You've already sacrificed so much. This could be a game changer for you, your mom, and Koti."

"Why do you have to be the voice of reason?" I grumble.

"Because, my friend, you deserve more than life has been throwing at you. Your sister's situation threw a monkey wrench into your life plans. Losing Olivia and her husband, being left eight months pregnant with their daughter, and drowning in medical bills - it's like a tragic rom-com with too many plot twists."

"I'd replay the tragic rom-com for Koti any day, even knowing my sister and her husband were going to be killed before she was born."

"I get it, Piper. But this is your chance to break

free from bill mountain and grab life by the horns, not just for you but for her."

I grit my teeth, conceding that she's right. "I'll mull over his offer; I just wish he wasn't such a jerk."

"It's six months, seven tops," she adds. "Maybe you'll find out he's not such the colossal jerk you think he is."

"I won't hold my breath on it. Why couldn't he be more like his sweet father?" I swing open the door to the bustling restaurant, filled with patrons and lively chatter. "I promised Koti a milkshake. I won't be able hear you in here. I'll give you a call tomorrow, scandal queen."

"Okay, but I want all the deets about your deal with the hot jock - don't skimp on the juicy stuff."

"Well, be prepared to be dazzled by the sheer lack of juiciness," I declare dramatically before hanging up the phone.

"I'd like to order three chocolate milkshakes to go," I tell the lady behind the counter. Stepping back, I take a moment to survey the hockey memorabilia displayed on the walls. A particular picture captures my attention with the title, "Seth Spencer was on his way to the NHL." The article beneath has been obscured by a photo of Seth in his hockey uniform, sparking my curiosity to delve into it later. I pivot around, drawn by a familiar grating voice, and spot Jake sitting in a booth with a strawberry blond woman, while his father sits across from them.

Seth notices me and waves me over. "Hi Piper. How did those boots work out for you?"

Jake, pointing between us, interrupts, "You two know each other?"

"Yes. After the embarrassing incident on the sidewalk, I made it on my own two feet to the outdoor store, where I met your father."

The young woman sitting next to Jake signs something with her hands.

"This is my daughter, Jewels. She says she thinks you're pretty," Seth states, smiling.

Jake reacts with a curled lip.

His sister, not another woman vying for his attention. "Can you tell her it's so nice to meet her?"

Jewels snorts, her hands in motion.

"She can read lips," Jake says, drumming his fingers on the table like I'm imposing on him.

"Would you like to join us?" Seth invites, scooting over in the booth.

"This is a family dinner," Jake grumbles and just when I thought the atmosphere couldn't get any louder, Jewels pinches the inside of his arm, Jake in response, produces a surprised squeal that could rival a cartoon character.

I'm on the verge of bursting into laughter, but I manage to keep it together.

"What the hell? Jewels?"

"I think she's trying to point out that you are being rude," I snicker, watching Jewels adding a playful touch tapping her finger to the tip of her nose.

I like her.

"Fine. Would you care to join us?" Jake extends the invitation with all the enthusiasm of a sloth.

I ignore him and address Seth directly. "Thank you, but I placed an order to go."

"You should bring your daughter here. She'd love it."

Internally groaning, I brace myself.

"You have a daughter?" Jake whips his head in my direction, making eye contact.

Saved by my name being called for my order. "That's me," I announce lamely. "Thanks for the invite, perhaps another time, and again, it was nice meeting you."

Jewels signs to her father, her lips pressed together in a smirk aimed at Jake. "She says she's sorry her big brother can be such a jerk."

Little does she know; I've already been on the receiving end of his Jake's-jerk-ism. *Perhaps I should slap the hashtag #Jakesjerkism on all his social media pictures.* I give my devilish shoulder companion a shake-off. It's tempting, hilarious even, but definitely a bad idea.

"Enjoy your evening together," I say, strolling away to claim my order.

Inside my trusty eight-year-old Hyundai, I insert the key, and it responds with a groan.

"Please, not now," I plead, bouncing my forehead on the steering wheel. "You and I have been through too much together to give up on me." She was my first splurge after winning the gold medal in the figure skating competition in the south. Sponsors were throwing money at me, and I proudly paid cash for my first set of wheels, thinking it was just the beginning for me. Three years later, my world crumbled.

My phone pings in my purse - probably Koti wanting to know what's taking me so long. I fish it out and see a message from Jake.

You look like you're having car trouble again. A smiley face accompanies the words.

I quickly look out the side window, spotting Jake waving from his booth at the restaurant. In response I fire back a text.

How did you get my number? I attach a smiley face with horns.

You were added to the contact list for the Arctic Wolves, he explains, adding a tiny person shrugging emoji.

My car is fine.

I turn the key, praying. She sputters twice and then comes to life. "Ha!" I cheer.

You have smoke coming from your engine, he texts, followed by a flame emoji.

What is it with him and emoji's? *She's cold, that's all.*

I know where you could get the money to buy a new car.

I toss my phone on the seat, put my car in gear, and slowly roll out onto the main street, thankful when I turn into my driveway.

Stomping through the snow, I wipe my boots on the welcoming mat, and the front door swings open dramatically.

"Did you bring me a milkshake?" Koti has her hands outstretched, reaching for the bag.

"Yes. There's one for me and Meme too," I confirm.

She dashes inside, tearing open the bag, finding a straw, taking an enthusiastic gulp.

"You might want to go slow..." I begin.

"Brain freeze!" she screams, pinching the bridge of her nose.

"Because if you drink it too fast, you'll get a brain freeze," I laugh.

"Did you eat dinner?" My mom asks.

"I was so busy, I forgot to eat. The milkshake will suffice," I assure her, handing her one.

"If you change your mind, there are leftovers in the fridge."

"What kind of trouble did you and Koti get into today?"

They share a mischievous look.

Koti presses a finger to her lips. "Don't tell her," she whispers.

"She's going to find out sooner or later," my mom warns.

"Alright," Koti whines. "You know how you said I couldn't have a puppy?"

"Yes."

"Or, a cat?"

"Please tell me we aren't the proud owners of either one?" I squint.

"We're not," she smiles.

"Koti," I say her name sternly.

"Meme bought me a hamster. She said it would be okay."

"He's the cutest thing, all fluffy and white," my mother adds.

"You bought her a rat?"

"Dorito isn't a rat," Koti scowls.

"Dorito?" I chuckle.

She runs to her room and comes back cuddling our new houseguest. "See, Mommy, isn't he cute?" She rubs her nose in his fur, then holds him up for me to look at.

He is kind of adorable. "Welcome to the family, Dorito," I pat the top of his tiny head.

"Don't worry, he eats table scraps," Koti cuddles him against her chest.

"Did a cage come with this furry little thing?"

"Yes. Meme helped me set it up in my bedroom."

"Okay, take him back to your room, finish your milkshake, and get ready for bed."

She skips happily out of the room.

"I thought it would be good for her. She doesn't have any friends here," my mom defends her decision.

"It's not like I don't love animals, it's just that I didn't want another thing to take care of up until this point in my life. But, you're right, a pet that doesn't have to be potty trained, or taken for a walk will be good for her."

"My thoughts, exactly."

"It's been a long day, and tomorrow will start early. I'm going to tuck Koti in bed and take a long hot shower. I'll schedule myself off around two so I can spend some time with Koti. There's an indoor trampoline place for kids downtown I want to take her to."

"I signed her up for ice skating lessons on Tuesday nights."

"Send me an invite on my phone so I can add it to my schedule."

"I will. Goodnight, dear."

"Goodnight, Mom."

After tucking Koti in and leaving on a nightlight for her new friend, I shed my clothes and let the warmth of the shower soak into my skin until the water turns cool. As I'm plugging in my phone to charge, it pings again.

I hope you made it home in that beast.

"Where did Jake find an emoji of a truck towing

a car?" I wonder aloud. I curl under the covers and text him back.

She's more reliable than you think, I type.

Immediately, bubbles appear before his response.

Have you reconsidered my offer? Why didn't you tell me you had a daughter?

I bite the inside of my cheek and swallow the lump in my throat, hearing Maggs voice in my head that I should reconsider it. It would solve our money issues.

No, and my daughter is none of your business. Why would I tell you? We aren't friends.

He takes a bit to text back.

I'm sorry I've been an ass. We could really help each other out. We could be friends, nothing more.

It's late, Jake, and I'm exhausted. I'll give it some serious thought, but I'm not making any promises.

Great! We'll chat tomorrow.

I blow out a long, deep breath. Can I seriously do this? What would I tell Koti? I don't want her forming attachments to someone who won't be a permanent part of her life. It's not fair to her. It's just one more reason why it wouldn't work.

6   JAKE

"Today's practice was brutal, man." Bohdi shakes, flinging his wet hair all over me.

"Dude, I just put a dry shirt on," I grumble.

"I swear, Coach Charlie is on a mission to push us to the limit before facing the Grizzlies on Friday night. And, by the way, your shooting still sucks," he remarks, smirking at me.

"Yeah, I know," I reply, exhaling loudly.

"I guess Piper didn't agree to be your pretend girlfriend," he chuckles. "My photo shoot with her the other day was a blast. She's really attractive, but maybe it's a good thing she declined. You wouldn't be able to keep it in your pants with her."

"I haven't given up yet, but you're wrong. She's the last person in this town I'd consider getting involved with. Did you know she has a kid?"

"Yes, she showed me a picture of her on her

phone. I suppose having a kid would be a good deterrent for you; you've made it clear you never want children. Maybe offer her more money," he suggests, pointing a finger at me before I exit the locker room.

I fully intend to head straight home, devour some leftover takeout, and retreat to my bed solo. As I walk past the bleachers, two familiar puck bunnies approach me, flanking me on either side.

"We've been waiting for you to come out of the locker room," one of them says, her voice carrying a seductive rasp. The other one tucks her hand underneath the belt of my jeans.

I twist away from them. "I'm sorry girls, I've had a long hard practice and I'm going home."

"We can go with you," they suggest, running their hands through the sides of my hair.

"Alone," I gulp. "I'm going home alone." From the corner of my eye, I see Piper snapping pictures and waving at a little girl out on the ice. "If you'll excuse me," I say, pushing past two pouting women to walk over to Piper.

"Hey," I greet her. "Is that your daughter?"

"Yes," she responds, cutting her gaze at me briefly.

"She's really talented. How old is she?"

"Four."

"There's no sign of a ring on your finger. Where's her father?"

She studies me for a moment. "He's not in the picture."

"So you are single?" I raise an eyebrow.

"Now you ask me?" she huffs. "Did it ever occur to you to find out before you asked me to be your fake girlfriend? Or, let me guess, it wouldn't have mattered to you."

"I don't date or sleep with married women."

"So you do have standards of some sort," she mumbles, releasing the camera to let it hang around her neck.

"In my defense, I had no clue that you were a parent until last night, and, if memory serves me right, you were introduced as Ms. Piper Malone."

She gnaws the inside of her cheek and focuses on her daughter, ignoring me.

"So, any thoughts on my proposal?" I ask, hopeful.

She turns to face me, blinking a few times. "I've thought about it, but if I agree, it will be on my terms."

"Okay, I'm all ears."

"No awkward situations. No other women on your arm or in your bed. We," she wags a finger between us, "won't be sharing a bed. If you meet my daughter, you'll be introduced as a friend only. I'd prefer you not interact with her at all, but for the sake of authenticity, she'll have to know you exist."

"How is this going to work if you're not crashing at my place? It won't be believable," I point out.

"That is your problem, not mine. I'll play the part in public, but behind closed doors, we can continue to dislike one another."

"Convince me you can at least pretend not to hate me in public," I challenge.

Suddenly, her face transforms into a sweet smile that reaches her eyes, and her hand gracefully glides to my bicep, then to my jawline. She steps on her tiptoes, her lips dangerously close to mine. I close my eyes, anticipating a kiss.

"I'm not going to kiss you, Jake, but I made you believe it. If I can fool you, then others won't have a problem," she says, her words dripping with sweetness as if honey were flowing from her tongue. Barely a moment passes, and she's back on her feet, throwing snarky comments my way. "I see that worked for you," her gaze drifts to my crotch.

"I'll play by your rules as long as you can sell the act," I reply, trying to keep up with her banter.

"Oh, one more thing," she adds, grabbing the camera.

"What's that?"

"You'll tell Charlie Robinson the truth. I'm not going to risk my job because he thinks I'm cozying up to one of his players."

"If it keeps me focused, I'm sure he'll be on board."

"Then we have a deal," she declares, snapping a photo.

"Did you teach your daughter to skate?" I ask, looking out on the ice.

"A little. She's mostly picked it up on her own."

"If you're so good, why aren't you out there teaching her?" I tap my knuckles on the plexiglass."

"I don't spend much time on the ice any more." A deep sadness settles in her grey eyes.

"Did you forget how to skate?" I challenge.

"You may be fast, but I can skate circles around you," she snorts.

"Prove it," I dare her.

She stashes the camera in her bag, disappearing for a moment. When she returns, she's sporting a pair of ice skates. After lacing up, she hits the ice, positioning herself in the middle of the rink. With a poised pose, she glides through a routine as if it were tailor-made for her. Gracefully, beautifully, flawlessly navigating every jump and turn. I'm utterly mesmerized by her talent.

"Her injury didn't keep her from returning to figure skating," Dr. Hensley remarks, joining me at the plexiglass. "Something else sidelined her."

She's spot on. Her injury seems nonexistent, and I can't help but wonder what led her to give up her career. Piper finishes her routine and skates over to her daughter, taking her by the hand. They gracefully exit the ice, and I hold open the door for them.

"That was amazing," I commend, genuinely impressed.

"You're Spence," the little girl beams. "Number twenty-four."

"Koti loves hockey," Piper keeps her hand on her daughter's shoulder.

"That's amazing," I crouch down to her level.

"I know the names of all the Arctic Wolves' players," she proudly announces.

"I can't believe you're only four years old," I chuckle.

"She's been around hockey since before she could walk."

"Me too. My father played. I think I could skate before I could crawl."

"I saw a picture of him hanging on the wall in the restaurant the other day. He never mentioned playing."

I stand. "It was a long time ago."

"Mommy," Koti tugs at her mother's hand. "Can we invite Spence over for dinner?"

"His name is Mr. Spencer..."

"She can call me Spence; everyone else does."

"I'm sure he has other plans."

"Actually, I don't." I lean in close to her. "What's the point in waiting?"

"Sweetie," she says, pulling out cash from her bag, "how about you go buy a drink and a bag of chips? I'll watch you from right here."

"Okay," she responds, taking the money and skipping off.

"I think we should ease into this. It's going to look rather obvious that it's fake if we suddenly start acting like a couple."

"And, I say, haste makes waste. Your daughter is obviously infatuated with me," I grin.

"She's infatuated with hockey, not you," she retorts, propping her hand on her hip.

"All I'm saying is, we have to start sometime."

"Hi Spence," a woman I've been out with a few times, winks as she walks by me.

"Fine," Piper snaps. You can come over for dinner."

I reach down, taking her hand in mine and I feel her resist flinching. "You better get used to me touching you in public if we're going to convince people we are a couple.

The woman walks by again, her gaze zeroing in on our joined hands, and she huffs.

"See, working already," I laugh.

"I dislike you so much," she sarcastically flashes a wide smile.

"Text me your address."

She whips out her phone. "Call Charlie before you step foot in my house," she demands.

"No problem. He'll be on board."

"Let's hope so," she rolls her eyes. "I'm going to

call my mother and see if she has enough food made for another mouth to feed."

"Wait, you share a roof with your mom?"

"Yeah. Any qualms with that?"

"It's odd, that's all. Maybe that's why your ex bolted."

She squints, ready to unleash a verbal storm. "Not that it's any of your business, but I've never walked down the aisle. And don't even think about throwing more at me or cooking up wild assumptions about me."

I toss my hands up in mock surrender. "Fine, but brace yourself for some personal revelations if we're embarking on a fake relationship."

"Fake dating," she corrects through gritted teeth.

"Even so, I'll have to field questions about you."

"Fake it like we're doing with this whole relationship charade."

"Clearly, I've hit a nerve." Her hidden stories fuel my curiosity about her. "We'll need to dish out some details about each other."

"Fine, I have one for you," she says, crossing her arms over her chest.

"Shoot. I'm an open book," I offer my most charming smile.

"What's your tattoo say?"

My smile falters. "One Life. One Chance."

"It obviously holds some deep meaning for you. Care to share?"

I rock my jaw back and forth. "It's none of your business," I hoist my hockey bag further onto my shoulder and strut toward the exit.

"Did I hit a nerve?" She hollers.

I'd normally unleash the bird gesture, but I have a feeling she'd chomp my finger off. "I'll see you at your house, *sweetie*," I holler back.

I dash to my apartment, speed-dialing Coach Charlie as I transform from sweatpants aficionado to a guy rocking fresh jeans and a button-down shirt. Breaking free from my usual Arctic Wolves logo-clad clothing. I lay out my strategy to coach to get back on track. He appreciates the update, but throws in a cautionary note about not turning Piper's heart into confetti. I assure him that Piper won't be casting any love spells on me, and I won't be alluring her with my irresistible charm.

I take one last look in the mirror. "I can do this." It will be difficult spending my hours not on the ice with her, but if it works, then it will be worth it.

"Guess who is coming over for dinner?" My four-year-old, who is far too grown up, squeals when we walk through the front door of the house.

"Who?" My mom chuckles at Koti's pint-sized excitement.

"It's Spence from Mommy's team."

"Jake Spencer," I confirm, giving my daughter a playful hair tousle.

"Oh, hubba-hubba," Mom fans herself.

"Trust me, his dashing good looks practically stroll out the door once you get to know him."

"Can he sit next to me, pretty please?" Koti pleads, pressing her palms together.

"How about you tidy up a bit and lend a hand with setting the table?" Mom suggests.

"Sorry for the late notice. Koti invited him without consulting with me first."

"No worries. We always have plenty of food, but thanks for giving me a heads-up call."

"By the way, there's something I need to tell you before he struts in here." I sneak a glance to make sure Koti isn't in earshot. "I've agreed to be Jake's fake girlfriend for the season in exchange for enough cash to wipe out all of our debts and then some."

She scowls. "Some kind of contractural agreement?"

"His hockey skills have been off, and he believes it's because women in this town won't leave him alone, even though he doesn't exactly discourage it."

"So, you're pretending to be his girlfriend to ward off his local fan club?"

"More like the 'sleeping with him' fan club," I state in a hushed tone. "All I have to do is play the couple card in public. It will be challenging, but we need the money."

"If it's just for show, why is he coming over for dinner?" Mom smirks.

"We've got to bond and make our fake relationship look legit. Plus, a girls gotta eat before diving into a fake love affair, right?"

"Spence is your boyfriend?" Koti appears suddenly from around the corner.

"Crap." I crouch down to meet her gaze. "No, we're just friends." It's a bit of a stretch, but she's only four, and I spare her the details.

"He's cute," she says, batting her eyes.

"Come on, help me set the table," Mom interjects with a laugh, rescuing me from my inquisitive child.

I hurry to my room, opting for denim shorts and an Arctic Wolves t-shirt, throwing my hair into a high ponytail and adding a touch of lip gloss. As I finish, I hear the doorbell ring, and Koti squeals.

"He's here!"

Making a mad dash for the living room, attempting to outpace Koti to the door, I fail miserably. She swings it open wide, head tilted upward, staring at him like he's the eighth wonder of the world.

He glances at me, then back at her. "May I come in?"

I walk over to Koti, put my hands on her shoulders, and move her out of the entryway. "She's just excited that we're entertaining one of the Arctic Wolves."

"Mommy, why are you wearing lipstick?" She tilts her head to the side and touches her pink lips. "I want to wear some too."

"I have no idea why you're asking me that, sweetheart. Mommy wears lip gloss all the time."

"Not at home for dinner."

Just kill me now. Jake's smiling like a kid in the candy store with an unlimited budget.

"Are you two going to let him in or keep gawking at him?" my mother yells from the kitchen doorway.

"I wasn't staring," I mumble, channeling my inner sulky toddler.

Koti takes Jake's hand and leads him to the small dining area. "You can sit next to me."

"This is my mom, Emma," I introduce her, and I swear her cheeks turn rosy pink. Does he have this effect on all women? What am I missing? Sure, he's handsome, but once you get past his looks, I just don't get the hype.

He smiles, and instead of shaking her hand, he goes in for a hug. *Classic charmer move.* "Thank you for having me over on such short notice. Your daughter and I have some business to discuss."

"Don't you mean your girlfriend?" Koti sits, rests her elbows on the table and props her chin on her knuckles.

"Hardly," he scoffs with a chuckle.

If death glares were a lethal weapon, he'd be sprawled out on the floor right now. "We're..." I tilt my head to the side, closing one eye, "we're work associates." He's been downgraded by his insult. *What's so wrong with me?* More importantly, why do I care. It's a business deal, nothing more. Why do I feel like I'm starring in a low budget remake of *Julia Roberts in Pretty Woman?* I am by no means sleeping with him.

"Work associates," he repeats, sounding like I hurt his ego.

"I hope you like good old-fashion spaghetti,"

Mom declares, placing a large self-serve bowl in the middle of the table. "And fresh-baked-garlic bread."

He rubs his hands together eagerly, ready to dig in.

"What about saying grace?" Koti frowns.

"Sorry," he says, suddenly on his best behavior, hands in his lap.

Koti initiates a rapid-fire prayer, and it turns into a spaghetti battlefield between him and Koti. I swear the guy acts like he's been surviving on nothing but kale smoothies.

"I don't get many home-cooked meals," he confesses, catching me staring.

"I bet your kitchen is more of a museum for take-out menus." Mom quips, handing him the basket of bread.

"When we have away games, it's all about take-out life," he admits, taking a bite of spaghetti, and I can almost see him drooling over it. "This is so good."

"What about when you're home? Do you cook?" I ask.

"Not much, but Jewels cooks a feast for the team on the Sundays we play at home."

"Jewels is his sister," I clarify. "She's very sweet." *Unlike her brother.*

"Can I come and meet all the players?" Koti is bouncing in her seat.

"It's not nice to invite yourself," I scold her.

"Sure thing," he grins. "They'll all be there this Sunday."

My laser glare targets him.

"That's if it's okay with your mother," he backpedals, realizing he's entered the danger zone.

"Maybe some other time," I explain. "Mommy will need to be there to work."

She pouts, "Okay."

Jake leans in, practically whispering against my ear. "It will be a good time to introduce you as my girlfriend. The press will be there." His hand snakes its way to my knee under the table, and I freeze at the unexpected touch on my bare skin. His hand feels like a hot pancake on a cold plate, sending more sparks through my belly than a faulty electric outlet.

I quickly reach down, evicting his hand from its knee residency and shoot him a glare that could melt ice.

He chuckles under his breath. "You'll need to get used to me touching you," he mouths the words only for me to hear.

Clearing my throat, and the lingering sensation he left behind on my thigh, I wipe my chin with a napkin. "There's a home game is Friday night against your biggest rivals. Do you ever get nervous?"

"Not at all. When I'm in the game, nothing else exists but the drive to win."

"Did your father reach the NHL?" I'm curious about his dad.

"He did." His voice gets gritty, and he swiftly changes the subject. "Do you miss North Carolina?" he turns toward my mom.

"I do. Montana's weather will take a little getting used to."

"I miss Aunt Maggs," Koti chimes in, slurping a noodle.

"I didn't think you had any siblings," he states.

"She's my best friend."

"Aunt Liv was her sister, but I never got to meet her." Koti licks the butter from her bread.

Mom and I share a look. "She, um, passed away before Koti was born."

"I'm so sorry. It must be difficult to lose a sister. If anything ever happened to Jewels, I'd be devastated."

"So you're close to your sister?" Mom asks.

"She's my best friend, besides my dad."

There's a positive quality - he's close to his family. "Has Jewels been deaf since birth?"

"Yes," and I get the feeling he doesn't want to dive into more family questions.

"Can I fix you a cup of coffee?" I offer, getting to my feet.

"I'd love a cup. Thank you."

Koti scoots into my recently vacated chair and talks his ear off while I whip up a pot of coffee. Surprisingly, he's a kid whisperer. It probably comes with the territory of having a baby sister.

As I bring in the coffee, Mom escorts Koti to her

room. There was some minor whining, but Mom's the reigning champion.

"She's a great kid, and knows a lot about hockey," he says, blowing on his mug.

"Do you want children?" I inquire, making him almost spill his coffee like it's some sort of high-stakes interrogation.

"What kind of question is that?" he sputters.

"We're supposed to be getting to know one another, or have you forgotten?" I raise an eyebrow.

He rubs his lips together. "No. I don't want children."

"Okay, what about marriage?"

"I don't want that either?"

"Who hurt you so badly?" I ask, sensing there's an ache in his heart.

"How about we discuss the basics, like how did you land the job with the Arctic Wolves organization? Or, what's your go to take-out? Perhaps your favorite color." He leans close. "Do you have any tattoos under this t-shirt?" He runs a finger under my collar, and I wonder if he thinks I have a secret map of Narnia inked on my chest.

"I'm not into ink," I say, resisting the urge to trace the words on his forearm. *Where the heck did that thought come from?* "I applied online, bombarding them with tons of photos I had taken with links to social media sites I managed. It took three months for them to finally throw me a bone.

And, just to satisfy your curiosity: Chinese food and navy blue."

"How did you fall in love with the game of ice-hockey?"

"My great grandfather was one of the first NFL players back in 1917 when there were only four teams. He played for the Boston Bruins. His stories became my bedtime tales, passed down from generation to generation. I just wanted to feel like I was part of something great."

"And, now you've handed that same love down to your daughter," he grins.

"Your turn."

"I got scooped up by the Arctic Wolves during my second year of college. Been traded a few times, but now I'm happily playing in my hometown. Thai food, and possibly the color of your eyes."

It takes me a moment to realize he answered the question about his favorite color. "You're not going to charm me," I declare, even though his answer sends a sizzle down my spine.

"I'm serious; your eyes are beautiful."

"We're not in public, Jake. You don't have to be nice to me," I sigh, picking up our empty coffee mugs.

"Fine, you're hideous," he bursts out laughing.'

That's the snarky Jake I can handle, not the one who has been sweet to my daughter. "I do have a big ask of you," he follows me into the kitchen.

"You want our contract to be in writing?"

"That's not a bad idea, but no." I rinse our coffee mugs in the sink, then turn to face him. "I don't want Koti to get attached to you, so please don't start a Kid's Fan Club without asking my permission."

"Fair enough. She just showed so much interest."

"She will hang on your every word if you allow it. I'll bring her to the games on my terms. By the way, my mother is fully aware of our agreement. And don't worry, she won't let the cat out of the bag about our fake relationship to the neighborhood gossip club."

"Good to know," his eyes play ping pong with mine.

"I have a theory on why your shot is off."

"We already know why, hence our agreement."

"I suspect there's something else holding you back and even though I've seen women ogling over you, there's more to it than that."

"You're my pretend girlfriend, not my shrink." He walks out into the living room. "Any other crucial details about you that I need to be aware of? You live with your mother and daughter, moved from North Carolina to take this job. Your best friend is Maggs, and your sister died before Koti was born."

That highlights my life, leaving out the tragedies. "That pretty much sums it up."

"And what do you know about me?" he points to himself.

I tap a finger to my chin. "Arrogant, charmer, has a great dad, sweet sister who was born deaf, doesn't want children, or the sanctity of marriage. Anything else, or is that the cliff notes version of Jake Spencer?"

He grabs his jacket from the coat rack where he hung it when he came inside. "Other than being a maestro in the bedroom," he smiles.

"That's a performance review I don't plan on conducting personally," I laugh, holding open the door for him to leave.

"Wait, you didn't meet Dorito," Koti comes sprinting into the living room in her pajamas, critter in tow.

"Is that a hamster?" He kneels down, cupping his hands. "I used to have one growing up."

She hands it to him. "He's so sweet and cuddly. Momma doesn't like him."

"I didn't say that I didn't like him."

"She thinks he's a rat," she rolls her eyes.

"This cute little thing?" He nuzzles it against his cheek. "Next time I come over, I'll bring him a treat."

"I don't think there's a need for a next time."

"Oh, there will be, trust me," he scoffs, returning the furry hamster to Koti.

"Good night, Spence," Koti says, beaming as she returns to her room.

"I think my four-year-old daughter is flirting with you."

"Just like every other woman in this town, except you. That's why this is going to work so well. There's no chemistry between us. Thank your mom for dinner," he kisses me on the cheek and dashes out the door.

"Yeah, good thing there's no chemistry," I mutter, sending a memo to my body to remember that.

8 JAKE

I'm kidding myself if I think there's no chemistry between us. She's drop-dead gorgeous and funny, even though most of her snark is aimed at me. The silver lining is, she doesn't like me, so there's no way anything will happen between us.

I head to my apartment to find Jewels curled up on the couch, watching a movie and munching on popcorn.

"Hey," she signs the word and waves.

"What are you doing here?" I shrug out of my coat.

"I wanted to spend some time with my big brother before you're jet-setting every other week." She signs so fast sometimes I struggle to keep up.

I join her on the couch and steal popcorn from her bowl.

"Were you on a date?"

"No. I've sworn off dating for the season. I nego-tiated with Piper to be my fake girlfriend until then."

"This should be interesting. She's really pretty."

"Piper is immune to my charms," I chuckle.

"So you're saying you're going to be sexually frustrated for how many months?" She laughs. "How is that going to help your game?"

"This is not a conversation I want to have with my baby sister."

"I know about your reputation, Jake. Everyone in town talks about it."

"Still, we don't need to discuss it." I settle with my arm around her shoulder.

"Bohdi's hot," she signs.

My head falls back on the couch. "He's not inter-ested. You're my sister."

"What does that have to do with it? You think I'm not attracted to a hot guy? Or, perhaps you're trying to protect me because I'm deaf. Just because I can't hear doesn't mean I can't have a spicy rendezvous in a man's bed." Her hands are moving at warp speed.

"Whoa! You're my little sister and you're still a virgin." I close my eyes, bracing for the sibling shockwave.

She plops on top of me, peeling open my eyelids. "I'm a grown woman who has needs."

"Needs!" I roll her off of me. "I can't hear you," I cover my ears.

Her whole body jiggles with laughter. "You're too easy, Jake."

"And you're not funny at all."

"Seriously though, he's smoking hot."

"I will murder him in his sleep if he even looks at you sideways."

"I'm betting by the end of the season, you and Piper will be picking out sheets together, and you'll be writing her love poems."

"Not going to happen, baby girl. I've got too big of plans to let something as trivial as love get in the way. This time next year, you'll be flying out to watch me play in the NHL."

"You don't have to worry about Dad, you know. He has me, and I'll be taking over the store so he can retire."

"I'm not worried," I lie, fidgeting in my seat.

"Good, because he wants this for you."

"Are you sleeping on the couch?" I ask, standing. She nods.

"I'll see you in the morning"

She signs, "Good night," and blows me a kiss.

IT'S FRIDAY MORNING, game day. So there's no practice, only a team meeting. My teammates, and all the other staff, including Piper, are gathered on the bleachers. I'm perched on the very top, leaning my back against the wall with Bohdi and Karter flanking me. Piper is sitting on the very bottom row next to Dr. Hensley.

I discreetly take out my phone and text her.

I'VE MISSED *your beautiful face.*

HER PHONE MUST VIBRATE in her pocket. She tugs it out. A few seconds later, she texts me back.

YOU'RE SUPPOSED *to be paying attention to Charlie.*

COME SIT BY ME.

THREE BUBBLES APPEAR.

NO.

YOU NEED *to play the part,* I respond.

. . .

I DON'T HAVE *enough coffee in my system yet to be friendly. Who calls meetings at five in the morning?*

CHARLIE.

I BET *he does those polar bear plunges. He's so enthusiastic in the morning.*

PART *of me is enthusiastic in the morning too.* I include a smiley face emoji.

She glares at me over her shoulder, and I chuckle.

AGAIN, *not enough coffee, and down boy.*

WHEN OUR MEETING IS DONE, *there will be reporters waiting for us to talk about game day. I need you by my side.*

HER ONLY RESPONSE is to shove the phone back in her pocket.

. . .

WHEN COACH WRAPS IT UP, the doors open and the local reporters come inside, followed by a group of puck bunnies. I make my way down to Piper and wrap my arm around her waist.

"Hey, babe," I smile.

"Spence!" A few girls yell for my attention.

Piper inhales and laces her hand with mine. "Let's do this," she says.

We walk toward the crowd of women and glares fall on our hands.

"Sorry girls, he's off the market," Piper states, angling her body to mine. She places a soft kiss to my lips, tasting sweet as honey. The scowls that ensue, tells me they are buying it.

I snag one of the reporters. "I want a picture of us in the paper. Front-page news."

"You with a woman, Spence, isn't newsworthy."

"It is when she's the last one that will be on my arm," I pull Piper close to me.

"Jake Spencer settling down? I don't believe it," he laughs, snapping a picture.

"Yep, I'm a one-woman man now. Isn't that right, honey?" I dip my head in for another kiss, and I feel the rumble of a growl against my lips.

"It's true."

"Prove it," one bleached blond woman snaps. "Tell me one thing you know about her other than the size of her tits?" she spats.

"She loves Chinese food, and her favorite color is navy blue."

She's the same woman I dumped last week because she was getting clingy. "It won't last long. He'll be in another woman's bed by next week!" she says, looking her nose down at Piper.

For the first time, I feel ashamed at my reputation, treating women as if they're disposable. "How about I buy you a coffee, babe?"

"I'd like that," she keeps her hand in mine and we go to one of the rooms that is set up for breakfast for the team.

"You go sit, I'll get it," I tell her, and watch her walk over to an empty table, that doesn't stay empty long. Remi and Brady strike up a conversation with her, and a protective feeling settles in my gut.

"I see you convinced her to play pretend with you," Bohdi jests, draping an arm over my shoulder. "When your deal is over, I might give her a ring."

"Stay away from her, and my sister," I growl, aiming my feet toward Piper. "Here you go." I slide the mug toward her.

"I don't know how you convinced her to be your girlfriend, but you're one lucky man," Karter barks. "Don't go messing it up."

"I want to go practice hitting the puck. Do you want to come with me?" I ask her, needing her away from my teammates. They're all good guys, but have one thing on their minds, well, two.

She stands. "Sure."

I grab my skates, and she tugs a pair out of her bag. "You don't have to go on the ice with me."

"I want to. I've been watching tapes of you last year compared to this year. You're hesitating before you're swinging your stick."

"No, I'm not," I grumble.

"You are. I can show you if you'd like." She pulls out her phone again, handing it to me. "Watch this," she hits play. "And now this one," she starts another clip.

She's right. "How did you pick up on that?"

"It's a skill," she smiles.

We skate onto the ice and I dump a bucket of pucks out, crossing beyond the blue line. After completing a few laps, I execute a shot, and it finds the back of the net.

She grabs a hockey stick and skates over to me. "That was too straightforward." She assumes a defensive stance.

"You're a woman. I can't face off against you."

"Shut the puck up, Jake."

"Okay," I snort, circling before aiming for the goal. She maintains position in front of me, skating backward. I attempt the shot, and she redirects it to the opposite side of the rink.

"You hesitated," she says, smoothly skating to retrieve another puck. "Try again."

We replicate the maneuver until I constantly hit my target.

"You need to do that in the game. Don't let whatever's in that head of yours take over."

"Nice work," Charlie says to her when she leaves the ice. "Maybe we need to hire you as a shooting coach."

As I exit the ice, two women are waiting for me. "Good luck at the game tonight, Spence. You still have my number, right?" She runs her tongue over the seam of her red raspberry lips.

"I'm in a serious relationship. I won't be reaching out to you anymore."

"You'll get bored," she tosses her hair over her shoulder.

The other one mimics hand gestures to call her.

"You weren't kidding, were you? Everywhere I turn there's a woman fawning all over you," she remarks, taking off her ice skates.

The sight of Piper on the ice has my frustration building. "I'm hitting the showers," I groan.

"A well needed one," she says, her gaze falling to my crotch.

I readjust the boys. This will be much harder than I think if I'm attracted to her. I need to go back to not liking her.

"Maybe you should stick to analyzing games rather than my manhood," I snark.

Piper's eyes narrow, a mix of surprise and something else flickering across her face.

"I didn't realize pretending to be my girlfriend made you an expert on everything," I retort, my tone sarcastic.

Her jaw tightens. "Fine, Jake. We should stick to our business relationship. No need for unnecessary complications. I was only trying to help you."

As she storms off, I can't help but feel a twinge of regret. The lines between our pretend relationship and reality can't be blurred. It will only resolve in tension, one that's building up in me the more I'm around her.

9 PIPER

"Just when I think he's a decent human being, his thoughts go off the rails," I vent to Maggs.

"Slow down, what happened?"

"He's...such an ass!"

"I gathered that, can you be more specific?"

"I helped him figure out why his puck handling was off."

"Because his head is on women?" She says the words slowly.

"No, not that. He was hesitating too long. And I'm starting to think it's really not his sexual escapades interfering with it. Something else has him distracted."

"It doesn't sound like he wants your help in figuring it out, Piper. You tend to do this with people you care about."

"Do what?"

"Try to fix things for them. That's exactly how you ended up raising a child. Your sister couldn't have children, so you had one for her."

"I do tend to do that, don't I?" I stop outside the outdoor store.

"Yes. Where are you?"

"I was thinking maybe his father could give me some insight to Jake."

"You're not going to let this go, are you?"

I sigh. "Fine, I'll let it go."

"No you won't," she snickers.

"No I won't." I swing open the glass door. "I'll call you later. Thanks for letting me rant."

"Well hello," Seth greets from behind the counter. Jewels spots me and rushes over for a hug.

"Hi," I smile.

She communicates something with her hands.

"I'm sorry, I don't understand, but I'd be eager to learn if you'd slow down a bit."

"She mentioned she's excited about the game tonight."

"It will be my first night capturing pictures of the team in action."

While Seth talks, she continues signing. "That, and she enjoys watching her brother play." He pauses, and she gives him a disapproving look, signaling him to continue. "And, Bohdi," he scowls.

"Ah, Bohdi is quite handsome."

She vigorously nods in agreement.

"He's too old for you," Seth grumbles.

She folds her arms over her chest, tapping a foot to the wood floor.

Their stare-down amuses me and I can't help but laugh. "I was hoping I could ask you some questions about Jake?"

"What kind of questions?" He comes from behind the counter, standing in front of me.

"He's been having a bit of trouble with his shooting and he attributes it to his...extra curricular activities, but I think it's much deeper than that."

"Was there a question in there?"

"I'm just getting to know him a bit; he's not real good at communicating, but I know he doesn't want children or a wife. What happened to him to make him feel that way?"

"Probably the fact that his mother left when he was five years old."

Jewels hands are moving again.

"I've told you a million times, it's not your fault." He runs a soothing hand down her arm.

"Why would she assume it's her fault?"

She gestures toward her ears.

"She left because you couldn't hear?" I furrow my brow.

"That was just an excuse. It was an ugly divorce and Jake remembers small details."

Jewels resumes signing.

"She believes he doesn't want children because he helped raise her."

"Jake adores you," I say, reaching for her hand.

"It wasn't easy on him. He spent hours at this store with his sister because I couldn't leave them home alone. He's the one that taught Jewels sign language. All his time was spent learning a language on his own and teaching his sister. When she was old enough to go to school, he took up hockey on the weekends. It was his escape. As a teenager, he worked here to help out, and I think he grew to despise this place. It took his childhood. When other kids were out playing, he was either here taking care of his sister or working. It wasn't fair to him. I did the best I could," Seth hangs his head.

"Why didn't you play in the NHL?" I gaze at him with sympathy.

"Because of the divorce. She didn't want the kids, and they had no one else."

"You sacrificed your dreams for your children. I'd say that makes you an honorable man and a good father."

"It jaded him. He invested all his passion in his love for hockey and hasn't formed any genuine connections outside this family."

"He's afraid of getting hurt," I whisper.

Jewels speaks with her hands again.

"She believes it goes beyond just fear of getting

hurt. If he gets picked up by the NHL, he'll feel guilty for not taking charge of the outdoor store and leaving us behind."

"That's the crux of it. That's why he's struggling." It's a lightbulb moment.

"I don't want my son to give up his dreams. While I'd appreciate him taking over the store, it's not his passion. Jewels aspires to it. He needs to release that guilt," Seth swallows hard.

The timer on my phone goes off. "Thanks for sharing with me. I've got to go. I'll see both of you at the game tonight."

I stop by the Arctic Wolves gift shop before I go home. Koti is sprawled out on the couch playing with Dorito when I walk in. "Hey, sweetie. I bought you something for the game." I toss her the bag.

She empties the contents on the sofa. "A team jersey," she cheers. "Do you think they have one in Dorito's size?"

"That would be a no," I laugh. "The fuzzy little critter isn't going to the game."

"Why not?" She asks with sincerity.

"Because hamsters aren't on the VIP list," I lean down, giving her a peck on the forehead. "Where's your Meme?"

"She's in the kitchen baking cookies."

"That's what smells so good." I move to the kitchen. "What kind of cookies are you baking?"

"Oatmeal raisin."

"Is there a special occasion I missed?" I ask, reaching over and popping one in my mouth, munching on its goodness.

"I thought you might want to spread some cookie joy, you know, hand them out to the players."

"Mom, they're grown-ups, not cookie hungry toddlers," I chuckle.

"Everyone succumbs to the power of cookies, dear." She shoots me a sideways glance.

"I have a solid hour to be productive on the computer. I managed to snap some killer photos, and before every game, I'd like to shine a spotlight on an individual player on the Arctic Wolves social media pages. Once I've worked my magic, we have to hustle to the game."

"That gives me just enough time to turn these cookies into tiny packages of joy."

"Please tell me you haven't assigned name tags to each bag."

"Okay, I won't tell you," she grins with a twinkle in her eye.

I log onto my computer and download the snap-shots from practice and the individual meetings I've had with all of players, minus the elusive Jake, who seems to have mastered the art of dodging my sched-uling attempts. The inaugural spotlight falls to Bohdi, and I can't help but smile, thinking about Jewels not-so-secret crush on him.

After my digital showcase, I'm in a hustle to

change into my game attire, opting for jeans and the mandatory long-sleeve, logoed shirt. I slip into the pair of boots I bought from Seth, leaving my long copper hair cascading down, and top it off with an Arctic Wolves patched-adorned beanie.

"Ready to roll?" I grab Koti's coat, and she's there, looking all kinds of adorable in her new jersey.

"Yep," she shoots me a smile that screams mischief, as she tethers a backpack to her shoulders.

"What do you have in your backpack?" I raise a skeptical brow.

"Just some snacks," she shrugs innocently.

"Lend me a hand, dear," Mom juggles a couple of boxes.

"Did you make enough for the entire season ticket holders?" I tease, holding the boxes while she wriggles into her coat.

"You can never have too many cookies," she insists, grabbing half the boxes from me. With my camera bag in tow, we head out the door, ready for the game and perhaps a sugar rush.

We roll up to the place and stroll in; Seth and Jewels are in a deep conversation with Jake. We walk over and I introduce them. "Mom, meet Seth and Jewels. Seth, Jewels, meet the mastermind behind my existence, and the mini me version. Emma and Koti.

"She's adorable," Seth states.

Jake throws a casual "Hi," my way.

"Hey. Let me get them settled."

Mom hands me the bags of cookies like it's the crown jewels and says, "Spread the sweetness, dear."

I let out a dramatic groan. "Mom, seriously..."

Jake catches a whiff. "Is that oatmeal raisin cookies I smell?"

"My mother thinks cookies are magical," I sigh.

"They are," Jake declares with a grin.

"She baked a batch for each of the players, and then some."

Jake dives into a bag, pulls out a cookie, and takes a mammoth bite. "These are all mine now."

I scoff. "You can't possibly tackle all those cookies."

He smirks. "Wanna bet?" And shoves the rest of the cookie in his mouth, looking like a chipmunk preparing for winter hibernation.

Jewels snatches the bag from him and throws some serious shade in the form of sign language.

"You never did learn to share," Seth interprets with a chuckle.

Jake attempts to grab the cookies, but Jewels out maneuvers him, and we all burst into laughter.

Mom, Koti, Seth, Jewels claim a spot on the bleachers, leaving me to pull Jake aside for a heart-to-heart. "

"Are you still in a mood? Because I don't think

your fans are eager to watch our first fight as a couple."

He closes the distance between us. "I'm sorry. I was being an ass."

"An apology? That's not what I was expecting."

"You were only trying to help."

"I think I know the real reason why you're having issues."

He silences me with his hand. "Can you just let it go for now? I need you to play your part."

I'm just playing a role, I remind myself. "Sure," I say, sealing my lips.

Hand in hand, we navigate the arena, with Jake taking time to sign autographs for the kids. I step back, observing the crowd's reactions. Some women wink at him, others lick their lips, eyeing him like he's a prime steak. A dedicated fan in his jersey number boldly hands him her phone number.

"He won't be needing that," I take it from her, tearing it to shreds. She gives me a disdainful look and grunts before strutting off.

"Hi Spence," another young woman coos, obviously enamored with him.

I lock eyes with her, wrapping my arm around Jake's waist. "I'm so thrilled to be your girlfriend," I purr into his ear, making sure she hears me.

"Jake! When will we be hooking up again?" Another lady hollers.

Jake looks uncomfortable, so I take charge. I put

my hands on his shoulders, turning him to face me, then cup his cheeks and lay a kiss on him. I'm caught off guard when his tongue decides to join the dance, leaving me breathless. *The kiss isn't real, Piper. He isn't kissing me because he wants to, even though in this very moment, it might seem that way.*

I lower my hands and head, bringing our kiss to an end. His hazel eyes are intense, fixated on my lips that now carry the taste of him.

"Spence, can you sign my t-shirt?" a boy's voice interrupts us, and Jake visibly shakes off whatever thoughts were consuming him.

"Sure, kid." He takes the black marker, scribbling his name and number. The kid's face lights up like he hit the jackpot.

Jake takes my hand and leads us toward the locker room. "I don't know what just happened back there, but I need my head in the game," he says, yanking off his beanie.

"It was just a kiss," I force out a lie. "You wanted it this way, remember? The women backed off. But, I don't think that's the issue with your game."

"I've got thirty minutes before I have to be on the ice. This isn't the time for your theories," he barks, turning in a circle twice. "Look, I'm sorry for snapping at you, and I really do appreciate your help. After we win today, we all meet at the burger place for a celebration. I need you there at my side."

To pretend, Piper, nothing more, I reassure

myself, "You can count on me as your fake girl-friend," I force a smile that feels more like a grimace.

He disappears into the locker room, leaving me alone. I proceed to set up my camera meticulously in a specified spot, poised to capture shots from every conceivable area.

10 JAKE

What the hell was that? That kiss sent shivers all the way down to my toes. It doesn't mean a damn thing. I've kissed my fair share of women, and yet, it was different. I craved her. I wanted to taste more of her. I ached to feel her underneath me. Even scarier, I wanted her *heart*. But don't even really know her. She has a kid, an adorable one, but a child none-theless. The only thing we have in common is our love for hockey. Besides, she despises me. I need to focus on the game. The kiss wasn't genuine, and I most certainly don't want it to happen again.

"For about ten minutes, you've been staring at that locker like it's personally offended you, bro."

Bohdi's voice snaps me out of my head. I lean down, lacing up my skates. "I'm ready," I finally mutter. "Let's do this."

"That's the Spence this team needs," he smacks me on the shoulder.

We head to the bench, and Coach Charlie delivers a last-minute pep talk. The crowd roars as the team hits the ice, music blaring. The goalie stretches and goes through his routine. Bohdi, Karter, and I pass the puck, warming up. The goalie stands poised. Karter sends the puck my direction and I sweep in with a shot that hits the bottom of the crossbar and goes right down into the net.

"Nice bar," Bohdi slaps me on the back.

It's the kind of play a goalie hates, but the crowd eats it up.

"How about you replicate that during the game," Karter razes.

The buzzer resonates, and we align on the blue line, hands over heart, awaiting the rendition of the National Anthem. My gaze drifts down to the ice, and, for the first time, I contemplate what lies beyond the blue line for me. If hockey wasn't my life, what would my existence look like? Would I remain in Summit Ridge? Perhaps take over the outdoor store?

As the anthem concludes, I take my position along with my teammates on the first line, at the center of the ice.

The arena erupts with energy as the puck drops, starting the game. The clashing of sticks and the rhythmic thudding of skates echoes in the air. My body collides along the boards, engaging in a struggle to seize control of the puck. Positioned strategically, Karter stands ready to receive a pass. I execute a precise pass, feeding him the puck, and he advances toward the goal. The goalie is masked and focused, tracking the puck's every movement, poised for the impending onslaught.

Amidst deafening cheers and taunts from the crowd, I swiftly navigate to my position in front of the goalie. Karter passes to Bohdi, who then relays it to me. I ready my stick, ready to take the shot, only to miss the goal.

"Damn it! The first few minutes were like a whirlwind of controlled chaos on the frozen battleground; that's where I'm placing the blame.

"Come on, bro! That was an easy one!" Karter's voice rings out in frustration.

The puck drops again, and Remi slides it to Justin, who stills the pucks forward movement, setting up the play. He passes it to Brady, who clips it to me. As I charge down the ice, the cold air whips against my face, adrenaline pumping through my veins. The puck glides effortlessly beneath my stick, responding to each calculated move I make. The cheering of the crowd in the arena drowns out everything but the sound of my own breath. With every stride, the opposing defenders close in, their sticks slashing on the ice in a desperate attempt to thwart my advance. As I cross the blue line, time seems to slow, it's just me, the puck, and the net ahead. With a swift deke to the left, I leave the defenseman behind. In a seamless motion, I could release a powerful wrist shot. My gut knots up, and instead, I pass the play over to Bohdi. He takes the shot and the puck soars past the goaltender's outstretched glove, finding the back of the net with a satisfying thud. The crowd erupts and I celebrate Bohdi's goal before skating off the ice, joining my other team-mates on the bench.

Coach Charlie scowls disapprovingly in my direction, shaking his head.

THE GAME ENDS in a win 4 to 2. Despite attempting more shots, my confidence wavers as I missed both opportunities. In the locker room, I hastily strip out of my gear, seeking solace under the hot spray of the shower. The weight of missed chances lingers, overshadowing any sense of our win today. Doubt creeps in, and I can't help but feel like I'm jeopardizing my chances of making it to the NHL. Frustration boils within me, cumulating in a forceful fist pounding against the tile.

"Hey, bro, we won," Bohdi says toweling himself off. "Your passing was on point. You'll find your mojo again with the puck. Figure out what's going on in that head of yours, and you'll be in the NHL in no time. I'll catch you at the restaurant," he adds, walking out of the shower area.

I take my time getting dressed to the point that everyone else is gone. I hear heavy footsteps behind me. "It was a solid game, Jake." Coach Charlie remarks, taking a seat on the bench beside me. "I get that you're being hard on yourself, but your plays for the team are crucial. Assists matter just as much as finding the back of the net."

"I doubt the NHL scouts see it that way," I mumble.

"Some of the top players in the league are renowned for their playmaking skills. You know this to be a fact."

"I just can't figure out why I can't bury the puck."

"Piper had some insights on that. Did you listen to her?"

"What the hell does she know?" I snap, standing up and tossing the towel in the basket.

"She's sharp and observant. It wouldn't hurt to hear her out. Your shooting can't get any worse," he chuckles, getting to his feet. "I'll expect you to put in some extra time on the ice before our away game on Wednesday."

Inhaling deeply, I step out of the locker room on a quest to find Piper. She's standing alongside her family and mine. Koti eagerly rushes over as soon as she spots me.

"That was so much fun!" She catches me off guard, enveloping my hips with her arms, her head barely reaching my belly button. You got 3 assists, 2 penalties, and that ref doesn't have a clue about slashing."

I playfully tip her chin up. "How old are you?" I chuckle.

"She knows the game inside and out," Piper beams proudly.

"Can you show me how to pass the puck?" She folds her hands together.

"I'm pretty tied up during the season, but you know who's a great teacher?"

"Who?" Her eyes widen.

"Jewels. She's very good at it."

Koti turns to my sister, signs a few words, enough for Jewels to catch on.

"When did she learn sign language?" I ask.

"She's like a little sponge. She watched Jewels communicate with your father, and she picked up a few things."

"I'm truly impressed."

Piper's gaze shifts behind me, and she throws her arms around my shoulders. "You rocked it out there on the ice, Spence," she says, batting her lashes.

Two women, who would typically be all over me, walk by without uttering a word.

"Thanks," I smile. My game plan didn't pan out on the ice today, but I'm not interested in any of the women right now. I'm happy in my fake relationship. "I still sucked in the goal department today."

"You know what? Why don't we forget about the game until tomorrow and lets go have some fun."

"I'm ready to hear your thoughts on why I can't hit the net."

"Tomorrow," she smiles.

"Mommy," Koti's voice sounds a little frantic.

"What, baby?"

"I think we have a problem." Her lips draw downward as her shoulders touch her ears.

"What's wrong?" Piper tenses.

"Dorito is missing."

"Did she say Dorito? As in her hamster?" I look between the two of them.

"Koti, did you bring him to the game after I told you not to?"

"He fell into my backpack."

I surpress a laugh.

"Okay, we'll spread out and look for him. You, young lady, stay with me."

We all disperse in different directions, scouring the bleachers, hallways, bathrooms, and every nook and cranny we can find.

I spot a tipped-over trash can and think, if I were a hamster, that's exactly where I would be. I search through the trash and see movement. "There you are." I cradle him in my arms and find Koti sobbing.

"I found your friend," I say, holding him out to her.

"Thank you," she cries, hugging him.

Piper squats down in front to her. "You're lucky Jake found him."

"I know," she says, crocodile tears streaming down her cheeks.

"Since you chose to disobey me, you're not going to the restaurant. Meme will take you home with her."

"I'm sorry, Mommy."

Piper kisses the top of her head and we go find our families. "She and Dorito are going home with you," she tells her mother.

Emma turns to Seth and invites him and Jewels over for coffee.

"I'd love to," he says.

Jewels signs that she's going to grab burgers with us. Which I take it to mean she wants to see Bohdi.

I grab my gear, and Piper casually tucks her arm on my elbow. I'm starting to enjoy her touch way more than I probably should.

"Do you mind if I ride with you? My mom is taking my car."

I pop open the back of my dark silver Audi Q5, tossing in my equipment. "Do you want to stow your camera bag back here, or keep it up front with you?"

"This is fine," she says, setting it carefully tucked in next to my bag.

"Nice ride," she remarks, climbing onto the leather seats.

"It was my first purchase when I made the team."

"I'm surprised you don't have a fancy sports car."

"This is practical. It holds all my gear," I shrug.

"You're like an onion, aren't you?"

I lift my arm to sniff my pit. "That bad? I took a shower."

She bursts out laughing, and it's a beautiful sound. "I mean, you have many layers to peel back. Some of them are surprising."

"Oh," I grin, starting the engine and driving out of the parking lot.

Piper shrugs out of her coat, and I nearly swallow my tongue. She's rocking a low-cut top, hugging her chest. I'd love to see her legs in a skirt. She's not overly curvy, a bit on the lean side, but her breasts fit her body nicely. Why have I not noticed how gorgeous she really is before? It suddenly feels really warm in here.

"These parties can be extremely loud," I warn her.

"Most celebrations are," her lips turn upward.

"The weather forecast predicts a snow storm coming in tonight. We probably shouldn't stay too long."

"I'm good with however long you want to be there."

"Did you capture some legendary shots of the

game?"

"Oh, absolutely. I can't wait to post them. I think Charlie is going to frame them and hang them in his office."

"He likes you and thinks you're sharp."

"He's a smart man," she grins, tapping a finger to her temple.

I parallel park a few blocks down from the burger joint, and then sprint to the other side to open Piper's door. I wait while she puts her coat back on, zipping her body inside.

"By the way, I like your top," I give her a cheesy grin.

"Showtime," she smiles, weaving her fingers with mine.

She feels good on my arm. I hold the door open, and noise floods my ears. Jewels rushes over and grabs Piper's arm, leading her to a table where Bohdi and Remi are hanging out. Piper removes her coat, setting it on the back of the chair and Remi's eyes dart to her cleavage, triggering a pang of jealously in me.

"Babe, I'm going to grab a beer. What would you like to drink?" I ask, kissing her cheek.

"Just a glass of water with a lime."

"Nothing stronger?" I ask.

"I'm not a big drinker, but thanks."

I make my way to the bar and lean on the counter-top, keeping an eye on Piper. Remi has taken the seat next to her and has inched it closer, and I don't like it one bit. I have no right to be jealous, but I don't seem to be able to stop myself.

I strut back to the table, carrying my beer and her drink, standing between her and Remi. "Do you mind if I sit by my dazzling, non-drinking girl-friend?" I all but growl, raising an eyebrow for added effect.

He huffs, rising from his chair. "My bad, bro. I didn't realize you two were a thing."

"Hey Spence," the waitress gives my shoulder a friendly squeeze. "What can I get you, handsome?" she winks.

"How about we grab something to-go," I suggest, reaching for Piper's hand.

"You deserve to celebrate the team's win," she declares, standing up. Before I realize what she's doing, she's sitting sideways on my lap. "I'll have a cheeseburger and fries. What about you, babe?"

"I...um..." swallow a deep indulgent moan, "I'll take the same thing," my voice comes out as pure grit. Then my heart decides to thumb furiously in my chest.

"Do you want to share your favorite milkshake?" She runs her nose along my jaw.

"You're really laying it on thick, aren't you?" I rasp. My complaint is for self-preservation. My jeans are playing a cruel game of how tight can we get, and with her on my lap, she's bound to notice.

"That was incredibly enjoyable; I can't recall the last time I had so much fun," I exclaim as I hop into the SUV.

Noticing the heavy snowfall, he suggests, "I should get you home."

In a series of practice moves, he maneuvers the SUV effortlessly from between two cars that were parked too close to his. Why does this skill of his turn me on so much? Perhaps it's the flex of his biceps beneath his shirt or the sleeves pushed up on his forearm, revealing his tattoo. I've never been one to find ink particularly attractive, but on him, it almost unravels me.

As I reflect on what I'm feeling, I realize I'm no different from those women that want him for his sexual appeal. I was initially put off by his arrogance when I first met him; I've come to see another side of him in the snippets I've learned about him since then. Beyond his cocky jock exterior, he's shown kindness by being sweet to Koti, despite claiming he doesn't want kids. Additionally, he took the time to sign autographs for the children eagerly lined up, wanting his name on their jerseys.

His affection for his father and sister is evident in every action. How admirable is it that he not only learned sign language but he also took the initiative to teach it to his hearing-impaired sister? It adds another layer to the complexity of who he is beyond the stereotypical jock. I contemplate what I might uncover if I delve deeper into his layers.

He parks his vehicle outside a tiny home community. "This is it," he declares. "It's not much, but it's mine."

"Here? This is where you live?" My mouth falls open in surprise. I had assumed he resided in an expensive house or an upscale apartment rental. His car likely cost more than his house.

He leaps out, hurries around to my side, and opens the door. I trail after him to the front step, waiting for him to unlock the door. While I thought my place was modest in size, his seems no larger than 500 square feet. However, when I walk inside, it appears spacious with high ceilings. The cleanliness is remarkable. I had anticipated a typical bachelor pad with clothes strewn across the floor and dishes piled in the sink.

"This is nice," I comment, removing my coat. He hangs up my jacket on a hook, and I slip out of my boots, careful not to track snow on the immaculate bamboo-colored flooring.

He removes his beanie, and his hair cascades down to his shoulders in waves. "This was my second purchase," he smiles.

"Priorities," I laugh.

"I figured I could always live in my car," he teases. "Would you like something to drink? I have a bottle of red wine."

"I didn't take you for a wine guy," I snort.

"I'm not, but my sister loves it and she buys me a bottle anytime she finds one she likes."

"You two are really close, aren't you?" I don't disclose what his father shared with me.

"Yeah, she's one of my favorite people in the world," he grins.

I take a seat at the two person breakfast bar facing the kitchen. I watch the strong line of his throat as he swallows a taste. I let myself truly look at him, reveling in all the details I'd missed before. I collect them in my mind like secrets. He has three freckles on his otherwise flawless skin, beneath his left eye. His bottom lip has a little dip in the center of it. His hair curls behind his ears.

"I think this one is my favorite," he holds the bottle up, reading the label.

I smile around the lump lodged in my throat

when he hands me a wine glass. I swirl my glass and take a sip. "Oh, this is good."

Jake leans on the counter, hazel eyes assessing me. He's temptation incarnate. "Your posts on social media were fantastic. You captured some good shots."

"You checked them out?" I ask, surprised for the second time tonight.

"Of course I did. I wanted to see how good I looked," he full-on laughs.

"Have you always been this cocky?" I grin.

His face grows solemn, and the weight of his words settles heavily in the air. "Most of my life, I wasn't sure of anything. Who I was, what I wanted, or how to get it. I was an insecure mess."

I gasp at his admission, a sharp pain of empathy clutching my chest. "How is that possible? You have an amazingly supportive father."

He comes around to my side, sitting next to me with a haunted look in his eyes. "It's the other parent that killed it for me. She left not long after my sister was born. Jewels wasn't perfect enough for her, so I surmised I wasn't either. I haven't laid eyes on her since I was five years old, but she made my dad's life a living hell. She tried to take the outdoor store from him, wanting everything he had, but her children."

The rawness of his admission is heartbreaking. I reach out, cupping his cheek in a futile attempt to soothe the wounds that run deep, leaving scars that time can't erase. "I'm so sorry, Jake."

His lips lightly brush mine with a soft kiss. "I feel like there is a pendulum swinging back and forth between us. One minute you despise me, the next you let me steal a kiss," he murmurs, his voice barely an audible whisper.

"I don't hate you, Jake," I reply.

His gaze intensifies, a ferocious heat that threatens to consume me. "You taste so sweet."

I lean back on the stool, shutting my eyes, bracing myself on my knees within the confines of his thighs. "I can't do this," I confess, my voice on the verge of a desperate plea.

As his hands run through my hair, I open my eyes. "Tell me why? Is it because of my reputation? I'll have you know, I've never brought a woman here before. Hotels or their place only."

"That's only partially the reason."

Understanding dawns in his eyes. "Koti." He exhales sharply and scrubs his hand over the back of his neck.

"I want you, but I can't risk turning this fake relationship into something more."

"Are you still in love with Koti's father?"

Tears well up in my eyes, my voice choked. "Her father is dead."

His gaze softens with empathy. "I'm so sorry."

"It's not what you think."

His phone vibrates, and he fishes it out of his pocket. "It's my dad. I'll call him back in the morning."

"No, it's okay. I need to wash my face," I declare, standing, not wanting him to see me vulnerable.

"It's in the very back," he points, and answers his phone as I retreat.

My hands tremble as water splashes over my face. Every time I revisit my sister's story, I feel nauseous. Hands shaking, I call Maggs, well aware of the late hour.

"Are you okay?" she asks, answering.

"Yes...no," I sob quietly so Jake doesn't hear me.

"What's wrong?"

"I'm at Jake's place and he opened up to me about something painful, and then he wanted to know my story. I let it slip without thinking that Koti's father is dead," I admit, sniffing.

"Oh, sweetie, you still can't talk about it without crying."

"I know," I wipe my nose with the back of my hand, and sit on the floor in the small space with my back against the shower door.

"Do you trust him?"

"No," I laugh through a whimper.

"But, I'm sensing you've changed your mind about him being a jerk."

"Yes," I blink back tears.

"Piper, are you alright?" Jake's soft knock echoes through the door.

"Dry up your tears, and when you're ready, tell him," she advises. "I love you," she adds.

"I'm so thankful you're my friend."

"Piper, if you don't let me in, I'm going to break down the door," his voice grows louder.

Without getting up, I reach the door, unlocking it.

When his gaze finds me, he bends down, engulfing me in his arms, carrying me to the sofa. He holds me, silent and unquestioning.

After my tears run dry, he rises and retrieves our glasses of wine. "I think you could use this, then I'll take you home."

I gather the parts of me that are unraveling and take two deep breaths before I polish off the wine.

He stands, staring out his front window. "I'm afraid we might be snowed in for the night."

Part of me wants to protest, the other part wants to be held in his arms. "I know why you're struggling on the ice."

He turns, leaning his hips on the windowsill. "Why?"

"You're afraid to leave your father and sister behind."

He doesn't react as if I've exposed a hidden truth; he already knew the answer. "They are all I have," he stumbles over his admission.

"If you already knew this, then why the pretense that it was something else?"

"I didn't want anyone to see through me. I wanted to give up on women. I hated how it made me feel not having a connection with them." His words hang between us, dripping with the bitterness of his internal turmoil. "I needed a way out."

I rise, approaching him. "Let me ask you something? Do you want to go to the NHL?"

"More than just about anything, but how do I leave them?"

"With your head held high. Your father and sister want this for you. Seth gave up his dream for the two of you. Do you actually think he'd want you to walk away from yours because of them?"

Our gazes lock, swaying back and forth for a long moment before he answers. "No."

"His reasons for giving up his dreams meant something to you and your sister. Your reluctance to leave them behind, although admirable, will only hurt you. Seth and Jewels will be just fine. Once that notion settles in your head, I believe your performance on the ice will return to its level from last year, if not surpass it."

He flattens his lips.

"Talk to your dad. You've worked hard for this. Don't let it slip away because you're scared."

He rises to his full height, wrapping his hand around the back of my neck, drawing me to his mouth. His kisses convey a multitude of secrets, each one with a distinct narrative. I crave to hear all of them. In my mind, the first secret is a desperate, *I need you,* lingering on my lips. The second, *a longing to absorb all of my pain,* a pain he doesn't even understand. The final secret, a fervent, *I want you, so badly*, manifested in hungry nips at my lips, pulling me closer to him.

None of those scenarios unfold; instead, our kiss concludes with both of us breathless, foreheads pressed together. "This is a bad idea. I don't want to hurt you," he whispers as if he's swallowed gravel.

I want to plead with him not to stop, to assure him he won't, but deep down, I know he will. "I need to call my mom and let her know I'm snowbound or she'll worry."

"You can sleep in my bed. I'll take the couch."

"Give me one more detail."

He sighs. "What do you want to know?"

"What does that tattoo mean to you?"

He nudges his sleeve further up his arm. "One life. One Chance. It's something my father used to say to me when I was younger, urging me to pursue my dreams. It used to make me happy, but as I neared my aspirations, it started to make my heart ache, contemplating leaving them behind."

"It's beautiful," I murmur, kissing his cheek.

12 JAKE

She lies in my bed, clad in my t-shirt. I've never wanted a woman so badly in my life, and here she is, underneath my sheets, without me. Restlessly, I toss and turn on the couch, aching with a need for a woman who needs more than I can give her. My arm hangs loosely over my eyes, shielding them from the brightness of the snow creeping through the blinds. The soft patter of footsteps on the floor makes me hold my breath.

"Jake, are you awake?" Her gentle voice instantly arouses me.

"Yes," I rasp, sitting up.

She settles on the sofa next to me, her hair a sexy, disheveled mess, and her long legs casually crossing on the cushion. "I couldn't sleep."

"Me either," I admit. "What's keeping you awake?"

"You mean other than the hot, tattooed hockey player lounging out here shirtless?" A playful smile tucks at the corner of her lip.

"Besides that," I chuckle.

"If I'm honest, I've come to really like you. You're sweet when no one is looking, and your love for your family is evident. You've got so much going for you."

"So why do you say these things like they are out of your reach?" I absentmindedly twirl a strand of her hair with my fingers.

"I lied about the reasons I gave up my figure skating career."

"Dr. Hensley suspected as much when she saw you on the ice. But, you don't owe me an explanation, Piper."

She licks her lips, her gaze fixed on her hands in her lap. I reach over, gently tilting her chin upward, urging her to meet my eyes.

"I wasn't injured," she confesses, her voice strained. "My sister Liv and her husband, James, couldn't conceive a child they so desperately wanted. They tried everything. I offered to be their surrogate, putting my career on hold." I watch as tears fill her eyes. "Everything was going great, and they were so excited. My pregnancy was perfect." She lifts the hem of her shirt, wiping her tears, exposing the soft skin underneath it, and a thin strip of white silky panties.

I groan inwardly. "Take your time," I say, my voice tender.

"When I was eight months pregnant, they were killed by a drunk driver."

"Jesus," I choke back my own tears, empathizing with her crushing pain.

"I was so distraught; I went into labor. Koti wasn't ready to be born and ended up in the NICU for two agonizing weeks before I could bring her home. Grieving for my sister, I found myself unprepared for the weight of motherhood. At twenty-four years old, I was faced with a decision I never thought I'd have to make - I considered putting her up for adoption."

"That's understandable," I murmur, taking her hands in mine.

"I was in what I thought to be a serious relationship with David at the time. I envisioned a future where we'd build our lives together. He didn't want children, and when I decided there was no way I could give Koti up, he callously abandoned me."

"Come here," I say, drawing her into my lap, aching for the weight of her heartbreak, and kissing away her tears.

"Let me be clear - I don't regret choosing her; she's my entire world. However, it hasn't been easy. I've sacrificed any resemblance of a life beyond her because I fear opening up to anyone. Both she and I have endured more heartbreak than someone her age should. I'm determined to shield her from any more pain, at all costs."

"I can't fathom the pain you've endured," I say, sharing in her heartache.

"But, if only for tonight, I don't want to be a grieving sister, a mom, or a woman that's been left behind. I want to feel something different, and I don't care if it's pretend."

I shouldn't succumb to the temptation to touch her, but her plea is irresistible. Standing, I take her hand and lead her back to my bed. "Are you sure?" My voice carries a deep, gritty undertone.

She responds by lifting her arms over her head, maintaining eye contact with me.

I feel like she's offering me a priceless gift, and I want to savor the moment, unwrapping it slowly and cherishing every detail. With deliberate care, I map exactly how I want to explore her. Where I want to touch her first. I can't believe she's here with me, granting me this intimate privilege. Affection, unlike I've ever felt before, wells up in my chest. I reach down, easing her shirt over her body, savoring every inch of her skin beneath it. I catalog her bare skin revealed with heavy eyes, my mouth suddenly dry, my tongue instinctively sweeps across my bottom lip.

I express the thought that's been incessantly circling in my mind, "How could anyone not want you? You're breathtaking."

Her fingertips trace a tantalizing path up the ink on my arm, and she whispers, "I want you."

My eyes snap up from the burning gaze I had on her breasts, and a full grin breaks out on my face. She reciprocates it with a smile and I feel like it's mine and mine alone. "That's the best thing I've ever heard."

Guiding her to the bed, I trace my finger along the silk of her panties, slowly dragging them down her long, lean legs. Gripping her ankle, I caress it, and widen her legs, making enough space for me in between them. Though I'm only touching her leg, every inch of my body feels alive. I squeeze her thigh and trail my thumb along the inseam above her knee. I hesitate when she arches her back and moans, like she's not been touched in forever. My palm traces to her hip.

"You have one more chance to change your mind," I growl, desperately hoping she won't.

She leans up, fisting my hair, and brushes a needy kiss to my lips. "My mind is made up."

"Lie back then," I urge with intensity. In unison, we surrender to the pull. The sensation of her lips on mine sends electrifying tremors through my very being, her arms wrapped around my neck. Fingers tangle in my hair with a fierce urgency that stirs a primal desire within me tracing a path of longing down her neck, I capture her rosy nipple between my lips, coaxing a desperate, throaty sound low from her. An undeniable truth hits me hard in the chest, I've never desired anyone more intensely in my entire life.

As my exploration continues southward, the absence of resistance fuels me. "Your tits are beautiful," I murmur, the vibration of my words caressing her skin, eliciting a sensual roll of her hips. My hands find their way to her belly, thumbs pressing in a bold sweep beneath the swell of her breasts. A breathy laugh escapes her as my hair teases her ribs, and I meet her gaze with a wild knowing smile. The sparks in her eyes intensifies as the tip of my nose continues its descent, my hands framing her hips with purpose.

Her fingers weave through the thickness of my hair, twisting and urging me to fulfill her unspoken need. I chuckle in response to her wordless plea, pressing further into her. As my lips make contact with her core, my hand glides upward along her smooth skin to cup her breast, fingers tugging at her nipple. An incoherent sound escapes her lips.

I eagerly strip off my constricting boxers, the energy coursing through me, mirroring hers. I'm practically vibrating with need, an itch that demands satisfaction.

Delving my tongue into her warm, wet core, I revel in her palpable shudder.

"Jake, I want you hard and fast, filling up every inch of me until the pressure is almost suffocating."

"I want to take it slow," I grit, my voice filled with determination. "I've got a plan."

Her hips wiggle with anticipation. "Care to enlighten me?"

"I'm going to make you come repeatedly, if you're on board," I reply in a husky whisper, sliding two fingers where she needs it most. A single circle and she chokes out my name.

"Jake."

I shift my hand and her nails dig into my back and I sense she's halfway there. I maintain pressure with my fingers while continuing my exploration with my tongue. Her hips buck, she tightens around me, and a breathy hiccup escapes. Lifting my head, I lock eyes with hers. "That's it, baby." I make her unravel twice before I reach for a condom, rolling it down my length.

Rising to my knees, I watch her face as I drag my hands over the swell of her hips and spread my fingers wide. She looks beautiful, a touch of wildness in her eyes. A bead of sweat working its way down my spine. My heart flutters. I slowly press into her and she wraps her legs around my waist. I collapse to one arm, kissing her like she's mine. A burst of pleasure sneaks up on me, licking up my back. I've never felt like this. Not ever. I thrust into her losing all semblance of control. My hands flex on her thighs, as my forehead grazes against her neck, the stubble on my chin leaving a trail on her skin. Pulling back, I roll my hips, and push inside, filling her completely. She matches my frenzied rhythm, urging my body into hers repeatedly, driving her up the sheets until her head collides with the headboard. She shudders, then freezes against me. Hands grasping, mouth working silently chasing her orgasm, drawing me in. My release comes with an intensity that leaves me breathless and exhilarated at the same time.

As we settle into the aftermath, soft waves of pulsing warmth surrounding us, I nestle into her chest, my body exhausted yet completely satiated. Her smooth palm runs down my damp back. Scooting up, I drop my forehead to hers and exhale her name. "Piper."

Her eyes flutter open.

"I hope you liked my plan," I tease.

"Every fiber of me loved it," she replies with a satisfied smile.

I WAKE to the desolation of an empty bed, the cold sheets mocking me in their solitude. Glancing at the clock, it reads seven forty-five. "Shit," I grumble, scrambling out of bed, realizing I have a mere ten minutes to be on the ice. I snatch my boxers from the floor and hastily throw on a pair of jeans, pulling on a long-sleeved shirt and yanking on a pair of boots. In a rush to grab my keys, my eye catches a note pinned to the fridge with an Arctic Wolves magnet.

THANKS FOR LAST NIGHT. *I didn't want to wake you. I called for an Uber to take me home. Don't worry, I know our agreement still stands between us. I don't expect anything more. Thanks for making me feel like a woman again.*

PIPER

WHY DOES her note carry a sting? We provided each other with what we needed. Our lives are on different paths. She has a daughter to take care of, and I have a career that will keep me on the road. It's logical, it's practical, it's better this way. Yet, an ache settles in my chest, refusing to be dismissed.

I sprint to my vehicle, tearing down the road and screeching to a stop in the rink's parking lot. Rushing through the doors, I quickly change clothes, lace up my skates, and manage to hit the ice, albeit two minutes behind schedule.

"You're late, Spence," coach remarks with a scowl.

"Sorry, sir," I respond, my gaze scanning the

arena, desperately searching for Piper. There's no sign of her.

After an exhaustive practice, I find my father immersed in the books in his office while Jewels waits on customers.

"Hey, Pops. You got a minute?" I ask, poking my head in the door.

"For you, always," he smiles, closing his laptop.

Shuffling nervously from foot to foot, I gather my thoughts.

"What's eating you, son?" he asks, adjusting his glasses.

"What's going to happen to you and Jewels if I sign with the NHL?"

"What do you mean, what's going to happen to us?" He chuckles.

"I won't be around. I'll have to leave Montana."

He removes his glasses, rising from his seat, meeting me on the other side of the desk, bracing his hands on my shoulders. "You've worked long and hard for it. I'd be proud of you."

"I know, Pops, but I'd be..."

"Abandoning us? Is that what you think?" His brows rise in question, sensing my apprehension.

"Yes," I exhale loudly.

He engulfs me in a tight embrace. "You're not your mother. I'm not your responsibility and neither is your sister. I'm sorry if I ever made you feel that way." He releases me, locking eyes with sincerity. "I will retire, and your sister will run the family business. I'll be able to travel to your games. I'm so proud of you, Jake, and I don't ever want you to give up your dreams for me or your sister. You've sacrificed enough. Hell, you've given us so much. You paid for your sister's college tuition, and you paid off my home. We owe you, not the other way around."

"That's what families do for one another. Neither one of you owes me anything."

"Fine, then you owe it to yourself to follow your dreams."

"You slept with him! Spill every juicy detail," Maggs squeals.

"Shhh," I hush, closing the bathroom door and muffling the phone with my hand. "Sleeping was just a warmup," I say with a smile, feeling a flush creep up my neck.

"You haven't had any action since that asshole, David dumped you."

"Believe me, I know. I'm just grateful I didn't forget the basics, like, what part goes where," I laugh.

"Thank goodness, it's like riding a bike," she snorts. "How many times did he make you come?"

"I lost count after the first round."

"First round!" she repeats rather loudly.

"He conked out, and I thought, why not explore? Next thing I know, he's wide awake, flipping me over, and we had brain melting sex. It was glorious."

"So what about the morning after?"

"I don't know. I left him snoring peacefully."

"You did the walk of shame," she's howling.

"I was afraid he'd think I was going to become clingy. I knew what I was getting into. I instigated it."

"You sly minx," she roars. "But seriously, good for you."

"It doesn't change anything between us. It was just one night of bliss, nothing more. Our agreement still stands. When the seasons over, I get the cash, and he's off to the NHL. Wow, I really do feel like Vivian in 'Pretty Woman.'"

"I saw the Arctic Wolves social media page. It was fantastic. Those jocks are quite the eye candy. I might just have to come for a visit."

"Speaking of the team, I gotta run. I need to shower and meet with one of the players for his one-on-one photoshoot."

After I'm showered and dressed, I hear Koti in her room chatting with Dorito. I step into her room to check on her. Her hair is a tangled mess. "How about I braid your hair," I suggest, picking up her brush and sitting on the edge of her bed.

"Okay, Mommy." She sits at my feet with her hamster on her lap.

"I have to work for a few hours today, but how about a picnic at the park later?"

"Can Dorito come with us?"

"No, sweetheart, and this time it's non-negotiable. It's for his own safety. You saw what happened last time."

"I'm so happy Spence found him. Can he come on our picnic?"

"Jake's busy, honey."

"Do you like him?" she peers up at me.

"We work together, that's all," I assert, though after last night, it's challenging to convince myself of such.

"I think he's nice."

"I'll grab some sandwiches and chips from the store."

"And cookies."

"Chocolate chip." I tie off her braid. "There, all done. You look beautiful."

"Thank you, Mommy."

"You're welcome." I press a kiss to the top of her head.

I SET up my camera near the goal, anticipating Brady's arrival at any minute. My heart pounds as Jake glides out onto the ice in full gear.

"Hey," he greets me, a dazed smile kicking up the corners of his mouth.

His gaze feels like a tangible touch on my skin, and the cool atmosphere suddenly warms. "I thought I was meeting with Brady?"

"I bribed him to let me take his appointment."

"Oh," I respond.

"You left my bed," his voice carries the weight of grit, and gravel, with shades of possession.

"It was time to go back to reality," I retort without meeting his eyes.

He skates close to me. "Am I just supposed to forget what you taste like?"

My insides tighten. "Yes," I reply after a few seconds, regaining my composure. "That's exactly what's going to happen. We had our fun, and it's over." I feel like such a heel.

He circles me on the ice, as if hunting his prey. "If you say so." He scoops up a puck with his stick and shoots into the goal. "I spoke with my father like you suggested. You were right. He wants this for me. Hopefully, my game will improve."

"I'm happy for you, Jake, honestly." An immediate image flashes in my mind - Jake on his knees, head between my legs, hand splayed low on my belly, holding me in place. His nose at my hip and my thighs pressing against his ears. I force myself to shake off the vivid memory.

"Thanks." His laughter echoes, devoid of any happiness. "Let's get this over with then. What do you want me to do?"

Kiss me, make me feel alive again. Pin me against the plexiglass. "Just take some shots at the net," I mutter, clearing my throat to disguise the ache within.

I snap a few photos, then switch to video mode. Jake lands shot after shot. He looks breathtaking like this, in his element, to the point where my knees feel like they might buckle. How did I go from not liking him, to...I don't even know what this is, but I can't allow it to happen. I have Koti to think about.

"Damn, that felt good," he smiles, wiping his brow with his sleeve.

"You looked great, too," I say, putting my camera away.

He skates closer to me. "Are we done?"

I can't help but feel like his question has a double meaning. "Yes, I have a date with a four-year-old."

A group of teenage boys skate onto the ice for practice. As we're exiting the ice, as usual, a woman with bright red lipstick, wearing a come-screw-me fragrance, slinks up to Jake. "How about I buy you a coffee?" she asks, batting her inch long eyelashes.

Jake seizes me by the waist, his hand settling on my lower back. "There's only one woman I want to have coffee with."

I have to will my brain to act. "You're the best boyfriend a girl could ask for," I exaggerate, grinning at the woman.

Jake's hand finds my face, turning it toward him, and he swoops in for a kiss, catching me off guard. It's more than a kiss; it's possessive.

I sense the air shifting, knowing that the woman has walked away.

"I've thought about kissing you all damn morning." He sighs, his hands pushing through his hair.

I sling my camera bag over my shoulder and make my escape as fast as I can.

I dash to the grocery store, on a a mission to pick up picnic essentials, including a few of Koti's favorite things. Picking her up from the house, we bundle up and drive to the park. She charges straight to the swings, leaving me to brush snow off a picnic table. There are a few other brave souls out in the cold.

Koti befriends a kid her age, and they conquer the jungle gym together. I take a few pics to send to Maggs.

"So, your date dumped you," a deep chuckle comes up behind me.

I glance over my shoulder to find Jake. "Are you stalking me now?"

He looks down at his sweats. "I'm out for a run. I happened to spot you sitting here all by yourself."

"Sorry," I offer.

"No, I'm sorry," he says, leaning on the bench.

"What are you apologizing for?"

"For letting anything happen between us. I should have had more restraint."

I blow out a puff of white air. "It wasn't your fault. I basically seduced you."

He sits. "I'm glad we're in agreement," he laughs, bumping me with his shoulder.

"I can't. You know that, right?"

He nods, bottom lip between his teeth. "I do, and I get it. You have to protect your little girl."

"So, can we go back to being fake lovers?"

He sticks out his hand. "Agreed."

"Good, I'm glad we talked," I force a smile, my words expressing acceptance, while my body harbors a sinking disappointment.

"Hi Spence," Koti waves, running over to him. "I thought you were too busy for a picnic?"

"I wasn't aware I was invited, but I'm never too busy for a little fun. What do you have in the basket?" he lifts the lid. "I don't think there's enough for three," he adds.

"I'll share my sandwich and chips with you," Koti offers generously, pouting for extra effect.

"How about one of those chocolate chip cookies?" He waggles an eyebrow.

"I draw the line at cookies," she declares, folding her little arms over her chest with all the seriousness of a four-year-old negotiator, and he erupts in laughter.

"That's alright, I'll settle for half a sandwich."

I shift on the bench and wince at the soreness at my core, and I have to blink back the vision of Jake thrusting inside of me, calling my name. Note to self:

picnic benches are not the comfiest spot for a post-passionate rendezvous.

The three of us dig into our sandwiches while Koti bombards Jake with her arsenal of silly jokes. He's surprisingly adept at handling her humor. I can picture him being an amazing big brother to Jewels, looking out for her. He's truly a good man, though he doesn't flaunt it for everyone to see. The mere thought of him leaving tugs at my heartstrings.

When he polishes off his sandwich, he dashes after Koti to the swings, pushing her sky-high until she squeals, giggling for more.

Don't fall in love with him, Piper. He's not yours to keep. He has a big bright future ahead of him, which doesn't involve a child.

He slows the swing down, and she jumps off, landing a bit too hard on her knees. "Ouch!" She cries.

My first instinct is to jump up and run to her side, but I stay put as Jake kneels beside her, offering her comfort and wiping off her leggings, rolling it up for a look. He helps her off the ground and guides her over to me. "It's just a little scrape, but it needs cleaning up. Do you have a first aid kit in that basket of yours?"

"No, but it's time to head home, anyway. I'll clean it up there."

"Can Spence come with us?" she asks, a stray tear rolling down her cheek.

He stares at me for a moment. "You know what? I need to finish my jog and hit the gym. Thanks for sharing your lunch with me." He tweaks her nose before taking his leave.

After dealing with Koti's scrape, we decide to embark on a movie marathon cocooned under a cozy blanket, while Mom who's multitasking with a book on her lap and achieving the impressive feat of being both awake and fast asleep simultaneously.

I glance down at Koti, only to discover her in a state of blissful drooling with eyes closed. Tossing off the blanket, I scoop her up and transport her to the land of dreams, making sure Dorito gets a proper dinner before I dim the lights.

Whispering sweet nothings to my snoozing offspring, I bid her good night. "You too, furry friend," I add.

Changing into pajamas, I curl up in my bed with every intention of falling asleep, my thoughts quickly take a detour to a certain someone named Jake. My brain conjures up images of him in various states - naked, sporting his hockey gear, rocking jogging pants, and let's not forget that tantalizing tattoo that served as a tongue tracing map last night.

In a desperate attempt to banish these mental snapshots, I grab a pillow and cover up my face, hoping the visions of him will go away. My mind refuses to comply.

Defeated, I resort to texting my confidante

Maggs, about my Jake induced turmoil. Only my fingers betray me, and the message lands in Jake's inbox instead.

I CAN'T STOP THINKING *about being in his bed.*

CUE internal panic and frantic attempts to undo the message.

BY HIM, *I'm assuming you mean me.* Smiley face. *You could come over and we could have a repeat of last night, or even better.*

GAH, I'm such an idiot. Mortified, I try to salvage the situation.

SORRY, *that text was not meant for you.*

JAKE EMBRACES THE MISHAP. *Then it's fate that you sent it to me. I was thinking about you, too. If you could see the size of my boner…*

.   .   .

STOP. *I don't want to know.* Actually, I do. I slip my hand beneath the elastic of my pajama bottoms.

ARE YOU NAKED? *I demand answers!*

NO, *I'm not, I'm fully clothed!*

I'M WAGERING *you're soaked.*

I YANK my hand out of my pants. How on earth did he know that?

GO TO BED, *Jake!*

DICTATOR MUCH. *I'm into it.*

AS I TOSS my phone to the foot of the bed, the room suddenly feels a few degrees warmer. My night has certainly taken an unexpected spicy turn. I kick off the blankets and roll to my stomach, determined not to think about him anymore.

14 JAKE

"I reserved you the comfiest seat on the plane," I declare, unbuckling the seatbelt.

"Thanks," Piper beams, stashing her camera bag overhead. "So, how stoked are you for the showdown with the Rocky Mountain Icehawks tonight?"

"I'm perpetually amped for a game."

"This is my first away game to cover, and I've never set foot in Utah."

"Well, be prepared to be dazzled by the glorious sight of an ice rink and the airport," I chuckle, reaching over to strap her into her seat.

"I must admit, flying first class is pretty awesome."

"Do you want something to drink?"

"I could definitely use some vodka mixed with orange juice. Flying makes me a tad jittery."

I reach over, holding her hand. "I've got you."

She stares at our entwined hands. "We're still playing our roles, right?" I whisper, sporting a mischievous grin.

She surveys the plane. "No one is giving us a second glance. They're all either glued to a screen or buried in a book."

"Alright, then, I'm officially terrified and in need of hand-holding."

As the flight attendant comes by, I place an order for a vodka concoction for Piper and water for myself. Piper retrieves a tablet from her backpack and a pair of Bluetooth earbuds.

"I was hoping we could chat," I suggest.

"Is there a specific topic on your mind?" she queries.

"Let's kick it off with that accidental text the other night."

"I don't think this is the ideal moment for that discussion," she replies in a hushed voice as the plane makes its ascent.

"Considering our recent conversation, I'm assuming you need the money for hospital bills from the birth of Koti. Didn't your sister and husband have life insurance policies?" I feel her grip on my hand tighten.

"They had a small plan. They were young and didn't anticipate dying. I used the money from the policy to establish a trust fund for Koti."

"Does she know about your sister?"

"She thinks Liv was her aunt."

"Are you going to tell her when she's older?"

"Yes, but not until I think she can handle it."

"I believe your sister would be proud of you."

"I'd like to think so."

"I'm still game for dissecting that text," I smirk.

"We agreed that it was a one-time thing."

"It doesn't have to be."

She remains silent in response to my remark. "Would you like to watch a movie with me?" she offers, handing me one of her earbuds.

"Please tell me it's not a chick flick," I grumble.

"No, it's porn," she deadpans, and I collapse into a fit of laughter. "Seriously, I'm all about action movies. I downloaded the new *James Bond* flick.

I snatch the earbud from her. "The musical opening alone could be considered porn," I grin, and she gives me a playful smack on the shoulder.

"You're such a guy," she snorts.

"I'm flattered you caught on," I tease, popping in the earbud.

As the movie unfolds, my mind wanders, consumed by the story she confided in me the other night. She's given up so much of herself for others, surrendering her aspirations, and I feel a profound sense of selfishness pursuing my own dreams. It seems wrong to crave more of her when she's sacrificed so much. Yet, I can't deny the magnetic pull drawing me to her. In the moments away from the ice, she dominates my thoughts. If I were a better man, I'd untangle myself from our agreement and maintain a safe distance. I am painfully aware that when the inevitable NHL contract comes my way, I'll vanish from her life. She'll become a bittersweet memory of the woman who captured my heart. She was nothing but temptation offering herself to me. Thoughts about kissing her occupy my mind incessantly.

Her fingers lightly graze my knee, and she smiles, saying, "You seem lost in thought. What's on your mind?"

"This," I murmur, leaning in to kiss her, savoring the taste of her sweetness.

She pulls away, locking her eyes with my lips. "That kiss...," she breathes.

"It's only sweet when it's with you."

The flight attendant interrupts our intimate moment as she delivers our drinks. Piper swiftly scarfs hers down, whether it's out of thirst or to cool the lingering flames from our tongues tangling together. I prefer to believe it's the latter.

When her movie wraps up, she switches to a book on sign language.

"I can be your sign language guru," I suggest.

"I want to conquer it solo, just like you did."

My heart skips a beat for this woman. "How about I school you in the art of dirty words?" I joke.

She laughs. "I doubt I'll need those for your sister."

"True, but the next time you're in my bed..." I waggle my eyebrows.

"There won't be a next time, remember?" she reminds me.

"That's a shame. I had a whole dictionary of naughty words ready for you," I recline, closing my eyes, disappointed but still amused.

Upon landing in Utah, we disembark and walk into the airport. I hold her hand, not wanting her to leave my side. When we make it to our hotel, I want her in my room, but she's five doors down.

"You can stay with me," I offer, whispering in her ear as she opens the door to her room.

"I don't think that's a good idea. You need to focus on your game and nothing else."

"Every single day since the moment I touched you, I've thought about you." I brush my knuckles against her cheek.

"I expect you on the ice in thirty minutes," Charlie commands, yelling down the hallway.

"Go," she urges, pushing through the door. We'll talk later. I've got work to do." As I turn to walk away, she reaches out, gently touching my arm. "Good luck tonight, Jake," she says, smiling sweetly.

I don't catch another glimpse of her until my blades carve into the ice. There she is, perched on the blue line, her camera aimed like a sniper, capturing moments. The national anthem echoes through the arena, a solemn prelude to the clash about to unfold. As it fades, we glide into formation. The Icehawk players are a formidable wall of defensive talent. My muscles tense, a mix of nerves and readiness, as I find my mark on the ice.

The game bursts into life when the referee drops the puck. Remi, a blur of determination and skill, claims the puck with the grace of a predator. The crowd's energy surges, a tidal wave of sound that drives out everything but the thud of my heart and the slice of skates on the ice.

Justin intercepts an opponent with a move as smooth as the ice itself, ensuring Remi's path remains unblocked. Crossing the blue line, Remi fakes a move to the left, leaving his opponent crashing into the boards. Positioned near the net, a breath away from glory or disappointment, I signal for the puck. With a swift move, Remi passes the puck between two players, sending it gliding across the ice to me. A flick of the wrist, I send the puck flying, time seems to slow, the puck spinning in midair. The goalie, a titan in his domain, lunges at it with his glove, missing it. The puck kisses the net.

The crowd explodes into cheers, and they chant my return. "Spence is back!" they scream.

The referee signals the goal. My teammates skate over, embracing me in a moment of triumph. In that second, everything fades away - the noise, the pressure, the weight of expectation. I am unequivocally, undeniably, back in the game. And it feels exhilarating.

The game continues with the first period ending one to zero. The second period becomes more aggressive, sending a few of our players to the ice, and gloves off for a few fights. Icehawks score one.

In the third period, with the clock bleeding down to the final minutes, every second pulses through me like a drumbeat of war. The score is deadlocked, the tension palpable. My legs burn from the exertion of the game. I catch the puck on my stick and a jolt of adrenaline courses through me. With the puck as my missile, I weave by the defenders, the goalie's eyes locked on mine in a silent duel. With mere seconds left, with a flick of my wrist, I unleash the shot, watching it hurtle through the air, slamming into the back of the net, just as the buzzer sounds. I've done it - scored the final goal, tipping the scales in the last precious second.

My teammates swarm around me with congratulations, and smacks on the back, almost sending me tumbling on the ice. Their faces are a blur of excitement, yet the crowd drowns them out. Amidst all of it, I search the arena for the one face that matters, but I don't see her. This victory, this moment of triumph - it's hers as much as mine.

IN THE LOCKER ROOM, the air buzzes with the afterglow of victory. Coach Charlie at the helm, his face filled with pride. "Outstanding game. You've toppled an undefeated team. Stay the course, and the Arctic Wolves are on a straight path to division glory, eyeing the Kelly Cup. Celebrate tonight, but keep it clean. We're facing them twice more before we return home. Any injuries, make sure Dr. Hensley sees you before you leave."

Celebratory high fives ripple through the locker room as we pack up our gear and head for the showers. Emerging refreshed, I find Coach Charlie lingering. "Your strategy out there was spot on. You played flawlessly," he states.

"Piper's the ace behind that. She really helped me to refocus," I admit.

He gives a knowing nod, his hand firmly on my shoulder. "I told you she was a smart woman." With that, he heads to the exit, pausing to add, "Keep up this momentum, and you'll be picked up by the NHL by the end of the season, if not before."

"Thanks, Coach, for having faith in me."

His laughter echoes back, a warm sound in a cool room. "Hearing you say that...seems Piper's done wonders for more than just your game. You might want to figure out how to keep her around," he remarks before disappearing.

How do I keep her and yet let her go when it's

time without crushing my heart? I feel like I'm walking a tightrope.

After toweling off and getting dressed, I opt for the solitude of the stairs, driven by a need to find her. Standing before Piper's hotel room, I knock, my heart racing as I press my ear against the cool wood of the door, and I find myself holding my breath until she opens it.

She instantly melts into my arms. "You were incredible out there, Jake. It's like you rediscovered your spark."

"Only because of you," I whisper back, the scent of vanilla in her hair grounding me.

"That was all you, Jake. You just needed to reignite your confidence," she says, pulling back slightly, and I immediately long for her closeness again.

"Do you want to come celebrate with us?"

"I wish I could. But I've got deadlines and I'm catching a flight back tomorrow for a meeting with the Arctic Wolves management team," she explains, a hint of regret in her tone.

Impulsively, I step closer, not ready to leave her. "Then I'll stay. We can celebrate the victory together," I say, edging past the door before she can protest.

"Jake, I really do have to work," she insists, yet her voice lacks conviction.

"I'll help. Besides, I want to see the shots you

took of the team," I offer, hoping to spend more time with her.

She snorts, "You mean your pictures."

"I want to see all of them. Justin, Brady - they were on fire tonight. It wasn't just me out there; their assists were game-changers," I argue, downplaying my role.

Her cute brow arches. "Since when did you start deflecting praise?"

"Maybe I'm learning from the best," I reply, drawing her close again, unwilling to let go of the connection between us, even if it's just for tonight.

15 PIPER

"What are we doing?" I hiss, feeling his lips trace a path of fire beneath my ear.

"If you have to ask, maybe I'm not as compelling as I thought," he murmurs, his fingers daring to venture beneath my shirt, flirting with the edge of my lacy bra.

I pull away sharply, creating a buffer between us as if distance could fend off the intense warmth radiating from him. "We agreed to not do this again."

"And why should we adhere to that? Give me one valid reason."

"Because if we cross this line again, I won't be able to imagine a world in where we don't collide. I made a vow to myself not to fall, not to let the shards of my heart be trampled on again. I can't - I won't - drag Koti through it. David turned my heart to dust, as if it were nothing but debris in his way."

"You're not debris to me; you're more than I ever anticipated," he counters.

"That's just it, you can't possibly comprehend. Your future is etched on the ice, not in playing house with a readymade family. If I ever let anyone in again, it's going to be with someone who wants children, someone who can look at Koti and see their world."

"What if I said I think I'm going to love you?"

"That's not enough." My words are a whisper, but they carry the weight of a thousand unspoken fears. Will I ever find anyone that can love both of us?

His shoulders slump, and he lets out a weary sigh. "At least let me hold you tonight."

"You have a victory to revel in. Wouldn't you rather be out celebrating with your teammates?"

"No," he insists, narrowing the distance between us, idly twirling a strand of hair between his fingers. "All I want right now is to be here with you, even if that means not touching you."

"You can help me choose which pictures from tonight's game should grace the Arctic Wolves website and social media pages." I really don't need his help. I already have selections in mind, but the truth is, I don't want him to leave.

His grin widens. "That sounds perfect." He takes out his phone. "I'm going to order room service. I'm sure you haven't eaten, and I'm starving. What would you like?"

"Just an appetizer will do."

"Yes, this is room 245. I'd like the bill charged to my room in 237. Two prime ribs with baked pota-toes, and whatever the vegetable of the day is, along with your best bottle of wine." Briefly pausing, he covers the receiver, "You mentioned an appetizer, right?"

My eyes grow wide and I shake my head.

"Add a calamari to that, thanks," he finishes with a smile.

"I've actually never had a prime rib," I admit in a hushed tone.

"Then tonight's the night you'll have your first one, courtesy of me."

"You shouldn't have. It's too much."

"Don't worry about it. I've got it covered, and I want it to be special for you."

Words fail me. It feels like an eternity since I've treated myself to anything luxurious. After David left, and the end of my skating days and Koti's arrival, my definition of luxury shifted to simply making ends meet, where Ramen noodles became a staple at our table. The idea of enjoying a steak seemed like a fantasy from another life.

I move toward my laptop resting on the bed. "Want to take a look?"

His gaze intensifies. "At the pictures, or you against the bedspread?"

I place my hands on my hips and give him a pointed look.

"Right, the photos," he quickly corrects, shaking off an image in his head.

I lift the laptop and bring it over to the small table by the window, taking a seat before he slides into the chair opposite of me. "Here are some of my top picks," I say, angling the screen towards him.

He scrutinizes them closely. "These are incredible. It's no surprise the Arctic Wolves snagged you for their social media manager. You actually managed to make me look decent," he says with a laugh.

But 'decent' hardly does justice to his appearance. Not too long ago, I likened him to Adonis, not just for his looks, but for his aura of arrogance and aloofness. Now, I'd classify him as dangerously attractive - so hot, in fact, I'd consider pulling the fire alarm just for the chance to have him rush over in a rescue attempt. *Pull-the-fire-alarm hotness.*

"I really like this one of Justin," he gestures.

"That's one of my best shots," I respond, my smile not just reflecting pride in my photography but also admiration for Justin's skill on the ice.

As we scroll through the images, selecting our favorites, the passage of thirty minutes is interrupted by a knock.

"Room service," announces a voice from the other side of the door.

Jake moves to open it, letting the server wheel in our order. After tipping him, Jake focuses on the wine, pouring us each a glass.

"To an unforgettable evening," he declares, offering me a glass. We clink them together in a toast.

"Here's to rediscovery of your spark," I say with a grin, taking a sip.

He places his wine on the windowsill and proceeds to unveil our meal, starting with the calamari.

My stomach embarrassingly responds to the aroma. "Turns out I'm more famished than I realized," I admit, tasting the crispy squid and relishing its flavor. He raises the silver lid from the prime ribs, causing my mouth to water.

Passing me neatly wrapped silverware in a white napkin, our fingers brush, and I feel the connection between us.

"Savor the moment," he says, flashing a dazzling smile.

My heart falters, pounding in denial of what I want, so hard it hurts. What am I going to do? The more I'm around him, the more I want things I can't have.

Throughout our meal, he unfolds narratives about his father's past, mentioning locations where he played hockey, describing his upbringing, and recounting how his dad eventually assumed control of his family's outdoor store from his grandfather. He proves to be a captivating storyteller, engaging with lively hand gestures and animated facial expressions.

When he's genuinely himself, without any facade, he's truly mesmerizing. I wonder if any of the women pursuing him have allowed him the space just to be, or are they only attracted to his exterior? "Have you ever been in love?" The question slips out impulsively.

He wipes his mouth with his napkin, then places it on his empty plate. "I once had a crush in high school, if that counts."

"I'm curious, I really want to know," I admit, fidgeting uncomfortably.

"No," he replies, offering no further details.

"It seems like you've had plenty of chances to find love."

"Women are drawn to me because I'm an athlete, or what they believe I can provide. They've never really tried to see who I am. I'm nothing special."

"I think you're special," I whisper.

"And yet, you're not interested in me," his look is piercing.

"I didn't say I wasn't interested, I am. What I said is that it wouldn't work between us because our futures are very different."

He leans back, taking a big breath. "Tell me about David. What made you fall in love with him?"

"He was sweet, and incredibly charming. I believed we had the same goals. He always told me he wanted kids until I was in labor with Koti."

"Have you had any contact with him since?"

"He reached out unexpectedly when Koti was two, pleading for my forgiveness."

"And you didn't forgive him."

"I forgave him, but I didn't want him back. He wouldn't be someone I could depend on, and I wasn't about to let him into Koti's life. The damage had already been done, and there was no going back."

"Without her, where do you imagine you'd be now?"

"I would have been an Olympic gold medalist, living in suburbia, likely married to a man who had fallen out of love with me."

"It seems you're better off now."

"Life's been tough, but I wouldn't change it for anything. Losing my sister was the hardest thing I've ever done. I was in a pool of grief. I didn't know how to get out of. In a way, Koti saved me."

He reaches over, taking my hands in his. "He was a fool to ever leave you, and I'm glad you're not in suburbia."

"Same here." I reply, intertwining my fingers with his, feeling that connection once more.

"I think it's time to retreat to my room and let you get some rest."

"Please stay." I know I shouldn't ask him, but I

don't like staying in hotel rooms by myself, never have.

"If I stay, I need you to be very clear about what you want from me. If it's open-ended, I'll strip you out of those clothes faster than I glide on ice and take whatever I want."

I gulp, a lump the size of a baseball forming in my throat. "I just want you to hold me."

"Naked, or clothed," he teases with a mischievous grin.

"I think naked would be a form of mutual torture," I respond with a playful wink.

"Can I at least ditch my shirt?"

"Not on your life," I laugh. "It's bad enough you're going to be barefoot. If you're shirtless, I wouldn't get a wink of sleep."

He rolls the dinner cart outside of the hotel room door as I put on a pair of sweats and a baggy shirt.

"You think that outfit's going to make me any less attracted to you?" he smirks.

"If you're turned on by this disaster of an outfit, then I'm pretty sure you've had one too many run-ins with a hockey puck," I snort, flinging back the bedspread.

"You know for us guys, all a woman has to do is show up, right?" he says with a cheesy grin.

I plop down on the bed. "If this is going to be too challenging for you, then you shouldn't stay," I sigh, feeling let down.

He tosses the blanket over me and climbs in beside me, wrapping me up like a burrito. "Challenge accepted. It will definitely be hard, if you get my drift." I burst into giggles at his playful pout.

Jake adjusts the pillow underneath his head and casually slings his leg over mine. "Do you realize it's just as difficult for me to keep my hands off you?" I murmur.

"You're free to touch me as much as you like. It was your rule that I couldn't touch you," he whispers, his breath warm against my ear.

He makes a valid argument, but how fair would that be? I roll over to face him. "You're not what I expected, Jake." I burrow my arm from underneath the cover, placing my hand gently on his cheek. "You deserve to have your dreams come true."

"And why can't you be part of those dreams? I never imagined I'd meet a woman who'd make me want more until you."

Beneath the blanket, I wiggle out of my sweatpants, and push everything out of the way, crawling on top of him. I kiss him as a wave of heat curls low in my belly. His fingers graze over my hips, touching me until I'm breathless, hands tugging at my shirt to free my breasts. Desire pulses hot between us, and I seize control until he makes a pure, unadulterated sound of relief.

16 PIPER

I can't believe how easily my determination to be hands-off with Jake crumbled. I had firmly decided not to fall back into bed with him. How did I get to like him so much?

I slipped out of bed when Jake was still sleeping, making my escape early to catch my flight. He was sprawled on his stomach, hair tousled, wearing a look of contentment even in his sleep. It took every bit of my restraint not to wake him with a kiss. All I could think about on the plane ride home was touching him, remembering the sound he made when I lowered myself onto him.

I force my eyes shut, trying to dispel the vivid memories before stepping out of my car. When I open them again, I'm greeted by the sight of a dark blue jeep parked in our driveway, pushing the thoughts of Jake to the back of my mind. Entering through the front door, the sound of laughter and the aroma of something delicious catches my attention.

Jewels is on the living room floor, cross-legged, with Koti, who has Dorito in her lap. They're communicating through sign language. "You taught her to sign," I say with a smile.

"Mommy," Koti beams, passing her hamster to Jewels before rushing into my arms.

"Hey, sweet girl. I've missed you."

"I missed you more," she replies, giving me a tight hug before scampering back to Jewels.

"Hi," Jewels greets me with a wave.

Emerging from the kitchen with Seth in tow, Mom announces, "You've arrived just in time for dinner," planting a kiss on my cheek.

"I had no idea the three of you had become friends," I murmur to her.

"I bumped into Seth at the supermarket. We started talking, and I invited them over to watch Jake's game with us," she explains.

"We thought it would be fun," Seth adds, smiling widely.

"I assumed you'd head straight home from the airport instead of going directly to your meeting. If you had, I would have informed you of our dinner guest," she says, patting my cheek.

"I had some last-minute photos to upload before my scheduled appointment," I explain. While I don't mind their company and appreciate their friendship, it feels a bit overwhelming, considering my current situation with Jake. *The question looming is whether my relationship with him is real or merely a facade?*

"Jewels and I are thoroughly impressed with your social media skills. I'm reconsidering accepting your offer for an online presence for the outdoor store," Seth states, placing his hand on my shoulder.

Jewels nudges him with her elbow and signs something, prompting him to continue. "Actually, it's Jewels idea. She'll be taking over soon and insists that we're missing out on sales because of 'my old grumpy self'", he adds using finger quotes. "She tells me I have to step into this century," he chuckles.

"I agree with her. And I'd be delighted to collaborate with you," I respond, addressing Jewels.

"Just provide me a cost breakdown before the two of you break the bank," he says, waving a finger between us. His phone chimes, and he retrieves it out of his pocket. "It's Jake. He calls me before every game," he adds, stepping away to answer the call.

"Mommy, I drew you a picture," Koti says, holding up a colorful piece of paper. It depicts a blue house with a tall tree beside it, featuring three people and what appears to be her hamster. "This is you and me holding hands," she points.

"And who is this?" I inquire about the man drawn beside her.

"That's Spence, silly," she rolls her eyes. "He's on skates, and that's a hockey stick," she giggles.

My heart stumbles through its next few beats. "You drew a picture of Jake at our house?"

"He's my friend," she says innocently, shrugging her shoulders to her ears.

Mom and I share a glance, and I decide not to make a big deal out of it. "It's a masterpiece. Thank you. I'll give it a prime spot on the fridge."

She skips off happily with Dorito in tow.

Jewels eyebrows knit together, and she starts signing rapidly.

"Wait a sec," I interject, pulling a book from my bag. "If you'll slow down a bit, I'll get what you are saying."

She obliges and I manage to decipher about every other word, needing to look up one to piece it all together. "Jake and I are friends. I don't want her getting too attached to him, that's all."

She signs again.

"No," I widen my eyes. "I'm not in love with him," I assure her, lowering my voice.

"Jake asked about you. He wanted to ensure you made it back in one piece, and if you were going to watch the game with us," Seth states, shoving the phone back in his pocket.

Jewels smirks and folds her arms over her chest.

"Dinner is ready!" Mom calls from the kitchen, rescuing me from any further questioning or sugges-tive looks from Jewels.

"Grab a plate, and we can kick back in the living

room for the game," Mom smiles, offering Seth a paper plate.

I cozy up next to her. "Are you flirting with Seth?" I whisper.

"Would that be a crime?" she bats her eyes. "I'm not dead, you know?"

"But, he's Jake's dad," I protest with pursed lips.

"Where do you think Jake got his dashing good looks from?" She gazes at Seth's backside.

This can't be happening. My mom seems to have a thing for the father of my pretend boyfriend. I have to end things with him, and this time for real. It's strictly a business deal, nothing more.

Shedding my shoes, I sit on the floor next to Koti, setting our plates on the coffee table. Seth and Mom claim the couch, and Jewels wedges herself into a chair. The players are announced and Jewels doesn't hide her enthusiasm when Bohdi hits the ice. They line up in their positions, and my mind drifts to what lies beyond the blue line for Jake. The answer is all about hockey - whether it's playing, coaching, or perhaps one day owning his own team. In the grand scheme of things, it definitely doesn't include me or a child. That's a sufficient enough reason for me to resist the temptation of getting into his bed again.

Koti cheers louder than anyone when Jake's slap shot finds its way into the net. We all laugh at how absorbed she is by the game.

"I think Piper is Jake's lucky charm," Seth suggests.

"He just needed to work out some issues, that's all," I dismiss his words.

Jewels signs, and Seth translates. "That may be true, but he really likes you."

"Jake and I are friends, nothing more, and when he gets signed to the NHL, I'll be there to support him, to see him off." As the words leave my mouth, I already miss him. *How did that happen?*

We witness the fast-paced clash of the game unfold. I gasp as Jake takes a brutal hit into the boards, anxiously waiting for him to get up. It takes a moment, but he eventually gets to his feet, visibly shaking off the impact.

Bohdi scores with an assist from Jake. As the clock ticks down to the final minute of the third period, the game is deadlocked at two to two. Just moments before the buzzer, Jake maneuvers in from the side of the net, skillfully guiding the puck past the goalie.

Koti jumps to her feet, hands in the air, chanting his name.

Jewels and I exchange high-fives, and when I look over my shoulder, Seth is hugging my mother.

"Can we call Spence?" Koti pleads, pressing her palms together.

"I'm afraid he'll be busy for a while. We can call him tomorrow."

She pouts.

Jewels signs, and I catch her conveying that in about fifteen minutes, Jake will text her phone. He always does after a game.

The more I discover about him, the more my heart aches. He genuinely loves his family. No wonder he was so messed up about leaving them that it affected his game.

I'm tidying up in the kitchen when Jewels walks in grinning, handing me her phone. She points at a text from Jake, indicating he wants to talk to me. Before I can protest, she hits his name, and his phone starts ringing.

"Hey," I say, softly.

"Jewels said she watched the game at your house with my dad."

"My mom ran into Seth at the store and invited them," I explain, though I don't know why I feel the need to justify it.

He lets out a long sigh. "I missed you this morning."

I grab my coat and step outside to chat with him. "About that, we need to talk."

"Can't you just let me enjoy what I'm feeling?"

"I made a mistake last night. It never should have happened again."

"I guess the answer is no," he half-laughs.

"Koti drew a picture of you with us at our house."

"That's sweet," he says.

"No. Don't you get it! She already likes you and thinks of us as family. I was very clear that I didn't want her getting attached to you."

The tone of his voice changes. "Because I'm such a bad guy."

"You know that's not what I meant. You have a future awaiting you outside of Montana. We have to stick to our original deal."

"A business contract," he murmurs.

"Exactly."

"If that's what you really want, I will need you at a press conference on Monday morning."

"Text me the specifics and I'll be there."

I hear him exhale.

"Jake," I rasp his name.

"I'll see you then," his voice is clipped, hanging up.

The front door groans open, and mom is wrestling her arms into her coat. "Is everything alright?"

"Yes...no," I choke out, laying my head on her shoulder. "I don't know what to do."

"You're falling for Jake, aren't you?"

"It was unintentional. The very last thing I wanted."

"I understand you closed your heart off to love after what happened with David, especially to safeguard Koti, but you're entitled to discover love again."

"Jake and I, it's impossible. I won't hold him back, and he's made it clear he doesn't see children in his future." I catch my breath, firming up my resolve. "No matter my feelings for him, I won't pursue it. Koti's well-being is my priority, not my own quest for a fairy tale ending."

17 JAKE

"Why are you down, man? You just got dream come true type news," Bohdi turns on his bar stool to look at me.

I quickly gulp down half my beer before responding. "I've never been rejected by a woman before. It's hitting me harder than I expected," I confess, polishing off half my beer and signaling the bartender for another one.

"Mark the calendar. Jake Spencer is heartbroken," he chuckles. "How did you end up brokenhearted from a fake relationship?"

"I don't know, man...she took me by surprise." I down another beer and tell the bartender to keep them coming.

"She is hot," he says with a suggestive lift of his eyebrows.

"There's so much more to her than her looks.

She's the most altruistic person I've ever met. And her daughter, who is adorable, isn't really her daughter. She carried her for her sister and brother-in-law."

"She kept the baby?" His brow creases in confusion.

"Her sister and husband died in a car crash when Piper was eight months pregnant with Koti."

"Oh, man, that's terrible."

"Right? She wasn't ready to be a mother, and she sacrificed her career to raise her."

He scratches his head. "I see what you mean about being selfless. She's way out of your league," he grunts, passing me another beer.

"Thanks buddy," I say, with a heavy layer of sarcasm, knowing he's spot on.

I've lost count of the beers we've downed, and my brain is swimming in a sea of fuzziness, and I've really got to pee. Stumbling off of my bar stool, I push past a table of women calling my name. I ignore them, not in the mood to get tangled up in their sheets. There's only one woman I want beneath me. Ducking into the bathroom stall for some privacy, I nearly perform a high dive with my phone straight into the toilet. With fingers that feel like they've been replaced with sausages, I compose a poetic text to Piper.

HHEYYY BOOTIFOOL. *I messsset u toonite.*

. . .

I SMACK the send button and lean against the stall wall, doing my best not to fall over as I wait in tipsy suspense. The screen teases me with those three little dots dancing and then poof - gone. Suddenly, my phone buzzes like it's possessed. Trying to answer it is like playing Whack-A-Mole with my face. After smacking my phone screen enough times to summon Siri's ancestors, I finally get it right.

"Jake, are you there?"

"I'm heeerre," I announce, stretching the words out like a loud drunk singer in a slow ballad.

"Jake, I think you have me on speakerphone. And you sound...are you drunk?"

"Drunkkk on luuuuve," I declare with the grace of a tipsy poet, my proclamation of affection bouncing off the stall's walls, entertaining an audience of absolutely no one.

"Jake, where the heck are you?"

"In the baffroom," I pop my lips dramatically.

"Are you hanging out with Bohdi?"

"Men don't pee togefer," I bounce my forehead off the wall.

"I'm going to hang up and call Bohdi. Please stay where you are."

"Are you commin to get me?" I ask, my head beginning to spin like a merry-go-round.

"Yes."

"Great, but can you pick me up rockin nofin but my shirt? Yer legs are pure magic."

"Jake, just stay put."

I squint at both my phones. "Piper." I bring it closer to my face, attempting to summon some focus. No luck. With a defeated sigh, my back meets the stall door, and I slide down to the cool tile floor, closing my eyes.

"JAKE, ARE YOU IN THERE?"

My head is throbbing like it's in a drumming contest with a jackhammer.

"Jake!" The door shudders against my aching head. "Move and let me in."

Ah, Piper. My brain decodes who it is. Bracing myself with hands on either side of the stall, I manage to stand, and the door swings open.

"You're a mess," she says, draping my arm over her shoulder.

"Where's Bohdi?"

"He wasn't in much better shape than you. I dumped him in the backseat of my car. Hopefully, he's still there."

She guides me through the bar, keeping me on two wobbly legs. I vaguely remember a chorus of women at a table calling after me.

"We'll take if from here," one of them declares, standing, shoving her assets northward.

Piper bulldozes her way past them. "I've got him. He doesn't need your kind of help," she snaps.

"A man like him could always use a hand from me, if you know what I mean," one of them chirps, and they burst out laughing.

"Leave him the hell alone," Piper seethes.

"Did you just say hell? I don't think I've heard you curse," I tease with a goofy grin.

"Shut up, Jake."

"Bossy, I like it."

"Duck your head," she declares, pressing my head down as if we're in a spy movie and not just getting me into a car.

"Hey, pal," I mumble, spotting Bohdi conked out in the back seat. "Shhh," he's sleeping, I hush, lifting a finger to my lips.

Piper slams the door, turning my headache into a drum solo. She takes the driver's seat, and I reach over, casually resting my hand on her thigh.

"Okay, Casanova, hands to yourself," she quips, firing up the engine.

"Where are you taking me?"

"To your house."

"Ah, to my bed," I grin, or at least I think I do.

"Not what I said. Bohdi's crashing on your couch. He's so tall; I'm not sure how he's going to fit."

"He can sleep anywhere," I slump down in the seat, laying my head against the cold window.

"WE'RE HERE. Can you manage to walk?" Piper pulls at my arm, and Bohdi is using my front door as a makeshift leaning post.

"My mouth's drier than a cotton ball," I say, getting to my feet with her support. "You're so pretty."

"At least you're not slurring anymore," she remarks, shutting the door, walking me to the front step. "Keys," she demands, holding out her hand.

"They're in my pocket," I smirk.

"I suppose you can't fish them out on your own."

"I could, but where's the fun in that?"

She dives her hand into my pocket, and I squirm. "You're not being very helpful," she growls, yanking the keys out and shoving them into the lock.

Bohdi stumbles inside, collapsing on the couch. Piper leads me to the bedroom. "Let's get you out of these boots," she says, sitting me on the edge of the bed.

"And you can work your magic on my jeans too," I waggle my brows. While she unlaces my boots, I manage to free one arm from my shirt but seem to misplace the other. "I've lost my arm," I mutter.

She tugs hard, and I fall back on the bed with a groan. "Please stay with me."

"I'll assemble a makeshift bed on the floor."

"I'm putting in a formal request for your immediate relocation into my bed." My eyes shut, and I detect a muffled chorus of frustrated mutters - either from her or my sleepy alter ego. Completely drained, I transform into a human burrito, basking in the glorious embrace of a blanket cocoon.

"Hey, Spence, aren't you supposed to be at a press conference in thirty minutes?" Bohdi's voice slices through my dreams like a caffeinated ninja. He gives my shoulders a vigorous shake. "Did you hear me, man?"

I squint open one eye. "That's not until Monday," I croak, my throat drier than a desert.

"This is Monday," he declares, ripping back the blanket like a magician unveiling a not-so magic trick.

I jolt into a sitting position, spotting a pallet of blankets on the floor, and suddenly, my hazy memories decide to make a grand entrance. "Did I drunk call Piper?" I scratch the side of my head.

"Yes, and I vaguely remember her playing designated driver to your personal circus, bringing us to your place."

"Where is she?"

"She left me a wake-up call on her way out, instructing me to drag you to the press conference on time."

I spin the clock on my nightstand. "Oh, crap! I've got only thirty minutes to make it there," I declare, leaping toward the bathroom.

"Isn't that what I just said!" he hollers. "The bigger issue is how are we going to get there? Our vehicles are stranded at the bar."

"Grab my phone and call my sister."

"You want me to call Jewels?" he pokes his head in the bathroom, grinning.

"Just for a ride. Keep your eyeballs to yourself," I aim a finger at him while brushing my teeth.

"You're aware that your sister is a grown woman perfectly capable of choosing her own dates, right?"

"In my mind, she's forever my baby sister, and I see it as my duty to shield her." A sudden realization sends a surge to my gut. Looking back on all those years of taking care of her, I wouldn't trade it for the world. It dawns on me that Piper feels the same way about Koti. For the longest time, I convinced myself I didn't want kids because, in many ways, I felt like I'd already raised one, missing out on my own childhood. My sister has been an immense blessing, and I've been blind to the fact that having a kid could be just as rewarding. I'm such an idiot.

"Jewels is en route. You might want to think about getting dressed," he advises.

"Got it," I reply, splashing water on my face and running a brush through my hair. Opting for a pair of sharp dark jeans and a grey button-down, I aim for a presentable look.

"Have you spilled the beans to anyone yet?"

"Nope. I've been keeping it under wraps for a surprise. Pops will be there."

"And your fake girlfriend. Lucky move, because once the local ladies catch wind of this, they'll be buzzing around you like a swarm of bees on a honey spree if it weren't for Piper. She'll create a no-fly zone."

Piper, her name swirls around in my mind, along with her smile, her body when it's next to mine, her touch on my skin. She's made it clear that our relationship can't be real, but my body is refuting it, and I want it to be, but how? She needs a man that will be in her life daily, not some athlete that will pop in and out of her life whenever he's in town. Why is it when you meet the perfect woman that life offers you the direction you've been dreaming about? I want her so badly, but she won't fit into my life. This is like trying to solve a puzzle with missing pieces, and it's driving me crazy.

"Jewels just pulled up. Are you ready?" Bohdi asks.

That's a loaded question. Yes, I'm ready to grab a

hold of my life's dreams. Am I ready to let go of Piper? No. "Let's go," I say, sidestepping his question.

In the backseat, I grapple with my thoughts, a mix of emotions swirling within. A month ago, I'd have no doubts about where I wanted my future to land. Today, it brings me heartache.

Bohdi and Jewels chat on the ride, smiling at each other. Bohdi is right; she's a grown woman, and I need to let her find her own path. I can see he cares for her - he's even taken the time to learn sign language. She looks happy, lighting up whenever she's with him. He's a good guy, and I've never known him to use women.

We arrive with just a minute to spare. My dad is sitting on the front row of chairs with Koti, a clear sign that Piper must be around. Swiftly scanning the area, I see her emerging from a side door accompanied by Coach Charlie, her camera hanging casually around her neck. As soon as our eyes meet, she flashes me a smile, and my heart skips a beat. She's dressed in a snug-fitting navy colored dress paired with heels that flatter her legs, she looks stunning. I mentally swipe left on the image of her shoes dangling from my teeth with her beneath me. It would not be great to have a boner while signing an NHL contract. No one wants a *rising star* in the wrong context.

Coach Charlie and I take our seats at the table,

accompanied by a signing coach from the other team. Piper, armed with her camera ready for action, stands nearby. The room is filled with my team- mates, local reporters, and a curious crowd of women.

"It's my privilege to announce that our local hockey player is being signed with the Mango Bay Mavericks, an NHL team out of Florida," Charlie declares with pride. "They're gaining not just an exceptional player but a top-notch guy. He's earned it with his hard work and killer skills. The Arctic Wolves team will miss him, but it's been a pleasure to work with Jake Spencer." Charlie gives my shoulder a firm grip.

"Thank you," I say, suppressing the lump in my throat. "I'm thrilled for this new adventure and grateful to everyone who's been part of my journey. A huge shoutout to my dad's wisdom and sacrifice - without him, I wouldn't be here. I'm excited about my future in the NHL."

A reporter jumps in, "When's the big switch happening? Are you finishing out the season here?"

"I'll play two more games with the Arctic Wolves before I pack my bags to Florida," I reply, stealing a glance at Piper, whose busy snapping pictures of my monumental moment, and the day my heart broke at the same time. She's capturing my highs and lows in a single moment.

I field a few more questions thrown my way. We

shake hands and I step from behind the table, fully intending to make my way to Piper, a group of women intercepts me, running their hands either down my back or my arms.

"I'm going to miss you, but you know where to find me whenever you're in town," one of them bats her eyes at me.

I glance over her shoulder, searching for Piper. "You know I have a fiancé," the word slips out before it registers what I've said.

"I thought she was just your girlfriend, a passing fling in your bed," another woman sneers.

Piper makes her way to my side. "He's taken ladies," she declares with a sweet smile.

"I don't see a ring on your finger," one lady tugs at Piper's hands. "He said you were his fiancé. Where's the ring?"

"I um..." she stammers, shooting me a scowl.

"You and Spence are getting married?" Koti emerges in the middle of them, clapping her hands.

Crap!

Piper grabs Koti's hand and whisks her away from the crowd.

"If she doesn't want to marry you, I will," another woman chimes in. "I'd love to live in Florida where it's warm."

"Excuse me," I assert sharply, determined to track down Piper.

Before I get very far, my dad pulls me into a hug. "I'm so proud of you, son."

"Thanks, Pops."

Jewels joins in, along with my teammates. "We're all proud of you," she adds.

"And jealous as hell," Bohdi grins. "But, I'll see you there soon," he gives me a hearty clap on the back.

I sign to Jewels that I screwed up and I really need to find Piper.

"This calls for a celebration. Lunch is on me at the diner," my dad declares.

Jewels assures me to go find Piper, saying she'll keep them occupied until I get there.

"Thanks, sis," I say, kissing her cheek.

I rush out into the ice rink and see Piper sitting with her arm around Koti, deep in conversation. Koti's head is down, tears staining her cheeks.

Debating whether to interrupt, I know I'm the cause of this turmoil, and I need to make things right. "Hey," I say, cautiously easing my way onto the bleacher next to Koti.

Her head snaps up, eyes red. "Why did you say you're marrying mommy when it's not true? You lied!"

Piper narrows her eyes at me.

"I'm sorry. I was nervous. I never meant to hurt you. I care a lot about your mother, and she's been helping me."

"I thought you were going to be my daddy," she cries.

Jewels comes out of nowhere and asks Piper if she can take Koti to the celebration.

"We can talk more about this later. I want you to go with Jewels, and I'll see you in a bit," she tells her daughter.

Koti takes Jewels' hand and walks away without looking at me.

"I'm seriously sorry. I just wanted them to leave me alone; I couldn't stand them touching me. All I wanted was you by my side." I run my hand through my long hair.

She gets to her feet. "This deal we have is over. I don't want your money. I'll work it out on my own."

I rise, standing in front of her. "I've fallen in love with you," I blurt out, then press my fist to my mouth, shocked at my own admission.

"I don't want to hear it, because even if it's true, you're leaving." She touches my hand, strumming it with her thumb. "I'm thrilled for you, Jake. It's the realization of your dreams, the life you've craved."

"I used to believe that until you came into my life. You've ignited a longing for something more."

"I know what it's like to give up your dream for someone else, and I don't regret it, but I don't wish it upon anyone else. What we shared wasn't even real."

"Don't say that. It was real for me. I've never wanted someone like I do you. I know deep down you feel the same way; you're just afraid to let yourself feel anything."

"This is tearing me apart, and it's not just my own pain I'm grappling with. I never wanted Koti to get caught up in our chaos, yet that's precisely what unfolded here today. I should have never allowed myself to get tangled in this mess."

She moves to leave, and I block her path. "Perhaps it was a mistake, but it brought me to you, even if only for a fleeting moment. I'll never regret the time we spent together; my fear lies in the possibility that I may never feel this way for anyone ever again."

"Jake," she says my name like she's a little dazed.

Taking her hand in mine, I lead her into the empty locker room, brushing a brief kiss to her jaw before swiftly moving to capture her lips. "I can't simply switch off what I feel for you. You've unleashed my emotions, opening my heart like a floodgate. I'm not ready to let go of you."

Our steps falter as her back meets the wall. "Those cursed heels of yours," I confess with a visceral desire, "I'm torn between wanting to tear them off your feet or witness you wearing nothing but them," I growl, consumed by an urgent need. Those damn heels have my thoughts dipping into carnal territory.

She rubs her hand down the back of my neck, frustration simmering in her eyes.

"I know it's selfish. Can we please find a way to work this out?"

The flush on her cheeks trips a shade darker. "I want to."

"That's all I need to hear," I hike her leg over my hip, pressing into her core. "I need you, Piper, more than you'll ever know."

I had never lived for the sound of a woman's throaty gasp before. My entire focus sharpens on her alone. It's not a mere need; it is a need, as vital as the air for my next breath. My lips graze her neck. What is it about the feel of her skin that has me nearly feral?

I try to protest, at least feebly in my mind, until Jake strips his shirt off. It's not like I haven't seen him naked before. In my defense, Jake Spencer's body demands admiration, out-right drool worthy. *Fire extinguisher hot* seems an understatement.

His stomach muscles, straight from a fitness magazine, that ripples when he flexes. My mouth waters imagining tracing my tongue along his ridges. The rest of him is lean and irresistibly appealing.

Jake's gaze levels on my legs, satisfaction curving in my smile with the way he's looking at me - like he sees me, not a mom, daughter, or sister, but a woman he desires.

"If this isn't what you want, you better stop me before I can't stop myself," he practically growls, sounding like a hockey player gearing up for a power play.

I respond by lifting my dress up above my hips, lightly grazing my lips over his, a teasing kiss that sparks every nerve in my body. He tightens his jaw, intensifying the kiss. His cool lips meld with my warm tongue, and his fingers spear through my hair, deepening our connection. I'm not a stranger to his kiss, but this one is different - he claims my mouth as if I hold the key to his next heartbeat, a blend of mind-blowing intensity, and a raw need.

After unzipping his dark jeans, he hooks his finger in my panties, abruptly pulling them aside. He lifts me, bringing us eye to eye, never breaking the kiss. My legs are wrapped around his waist, heels locked in place as he thrusts inside of me. I want him, even if this is the last time. He thrusts over and over, sending me spiraling. Every line in his body is tight against me, his breath ragged. I lace my fingers behind his neck as he rides out his wave of pleasure.

"Shit," he swears, ripping his mouth from me, resting his forehead against mine. "I'm sorry. I'm sure that's not what you were expecting."

"Overwhelming chemistry," I pant.

He eases me down to the floor. "I don't want this to end," he murmurs, his hand gliding down my spine.

"I wish it didn't have to," I reply, studying his face, etching it into my memory.

"All I want to do is drag you into my bed, block out the world, intimately explore every inch of your body, and relish the sound of your voice growing hoarse from screaming my name, fully aware that I'm the reason behind it."

Tears fill my eyes, and my lip trembles. "I can't, Jake," I say, as I hastily fix my dress. The click of my heels echoes loudly against the tile floor as I run out of the locker room, not stopping until the biting cold air slaps me in the face.

I slump into my car, swiping at my tears in the rearview mirror. "Why is it I always want the things I can't have?" I sniff. "Will there ever be a time my life plays out like I want it to?" Shutting my eyes, I push the mirror away. It's wrong of me to think that way. I've got a good life - a loving, supportive mother, an adorable daughter. I shouldn't need or want anything else...but I do, and his name is Jake Spencer. The NHL player destined to move forward, as he rightfully should. I'm genuinely happy for him; that's where my attention must lie. He earned this. He'll get over what he's feeling for me, and I'll become a distant memory. The issue is, I won't forget him - ever.

I'm stuck, no way around it. I have to attend the celebration and take photos. So, I'll slap on a smile and power through it, but not before calling Maggs.

She picks up on the second ring. "Hey, Piper."

My tears fall like a dam collapsing. "Oh, Maggs," I bawl.

"What's wrong?" Concern drips from her voice.

"I'm such a colossal idiot. I swore I wouldn't fall in love again..."

"With Jake?"

"He's NHL bound, off to sunny Florida."

"I could call them and tell them he's a terrible hockey player," she suggests, and I burst into laughter amid my sobs.

"They've seen him play; they'd never buy it."

"Okay, new plan; I'll convince them he's irreplaceable, that you're hopelessly addicted to him, and he's a wizard in the bedroom. But, quick check, is he any good in bed? Because if not, you can totally survive without him."

"This is why you're my best friend. You manage to make me laugh in my toughest moments," I say, wiping away my tears.

"But on a serious note, how about I catch a flight, and we have some quality time, you, me and Koti?"

"I'd like that."

"Great! I'll book a flight and send you the deets. By the way, I'm not into long-term relationships, so maybe you could set me up with one of those players. I'm more of a one-night-stand kind of gal."

I grin, fully aware her claim is far from the truth. She's weathered heartbreak and hasn't ventured into the dating scene since. We've collectively wallowed in the aftermath of heartbreak together. "I'll put my match-making skills to work and find you the perfect player. Thanks for being my shoulder to cry on."

"You've been there for me too," she sighs.

"I gotta go take some photos of the star player while holding it together."

I quickly check the mirror, ensuring no mascara streaks mar my cheeks. Straightening my spine, and summoning all the courage I can muster, I enter the lively celebration already in full swing.

Jake, who appears nothing like the man who moments ago had my back pinned to the wall, stands at the head of the table, raising a toast to his team-mates. When our gazes meet, he crosses his arms over his chest, mirroring a stance I didn't realize I had adopted. He pulls off the look much better than I do. There's a pang of rejection on his face that tugs at my heart. He eventually relents, running his hand through his thick curls, exhaling slowly.

His sigh seeps into every part of me until it feels like my own, a prelude to the impending heartache I know is coming.

"I want to take pictures, Mommy," Koti insists, tugging at my arm.

I crouch down to look her in the eye. "Are you okay?"

The corners of her mouth dip downwards as she shrugs one shoulder. "I'm sad Spence is leaving."

"Me too, baby," I brush my fingers through her hair and plant a kiss on her forehead. Standing, I suggest, "Let's set up at the end of the table to get some great shots of Jake and the team."

She slips her hand into mine, and I guide her to where I believe will be the ideal spot to snap the best pictures. After allowing her to take a few shots, I seize the opportunity to capture some for our social media pages. Once satisfied, I let her continue clicking until her interest wanes. Handing me the camera, she rushes off to Jake, who surprises me by picking her up.

Though I can't hear their conversation over the restaurant noise, the sight of Koti belly laughing warms my heart.

"Jake has always been great with kids," Seth remarks, wrapping his arm around my shoulder.

"You probably played a role in that."

"I did my best considering circumstances, but I wasn't as present as I should have been. He practically raised Jewels on his own."

"You did something right; they are both good people."

"Jake lost his way for a bit, but I think you helped him find his path. You've been a positive influence on him."

"All I did was help him uncover the reason behind his struggle. He took it from there."

"Well, he owes you for landing that NHL contract."

"That was all him," I smile, but it doesn't feel real.

Jake strolls over to where we are standing,

placing Koti on her feet. She runs off to Jewels. "She's a sweet kid, and for a four-year-old, she's incredibly smart," Jake comments, casually slipping his hands into his pockets. It seems like a defensive move, as if he's avoiding any temptation to reach out and touch me.

A brunette woman, who I've noticed swooning over Jake, links her hand on his elbow. "I'm so proud of your son," she tells Seth, smacking her lips. Jake's gaze remains fixed on me.

"Shall we go have our own celebration?" she asks Jake, tucking a strand of hair sensually behind his ear.

I'm on the verge of declaring he's mine, but I bite my tongue. Instead, I shoot the woman a glare that requires a four letter word to express my true feelings.

"How do you feel about that, Piper?" Jake's tone is flat, his stare intense.

"You're a free man," I respond, my throat threatening to close up as my body acknowledges the impending loss.

His stare narrows, and his jaw visibly clenches. "A private celebration it is, then," he declares, and the woman on his arm tightens her grip, smacking a kiss on his cheek that leaves a bright red lipstick stain in its wake.

He walks away, his spine rigid, and she clings to him like a shadow.

"I'm sorry, Piper. I thought perhaps you and Jake had something going on between the two of you," Seth says, a hint of sadness in his eyes.

"We're friends," I force a smile. "Jake is pursuing his dreams, and that's all that truly matters. If you'll excuse me, I need to get Koti home," I hurry away before my tears threaten to fall again.

I've been attempting to emulate a covert operation, dodging Jake since the day of his celebration. The mere idea of facing him after he sauntered off with that puck bunny is too much to bear. Sure, I practically gift-wrapped him for her, but he could have put up a fight. Instead, he opted for the stroll away strategy. Or at least, that's the story I've been spinning in my own head.

Here I am, stuck in the airport, playing the waiting game for Maggs' grand entrance to Montana. Thanks to a snowstorm, her flight is fashionably two hours late. Now, I'm in for a chaotic sprint to make it to Jake's last game with the Arctic Wolves on time. My stomach is hosting a full-blown butterfly convention at the idea of catching Jake before his final showdown on the ice. The thought of not sending him off on a happy note is nibbling at my nerves like a persistent chipmunk.

Maggs charges out of the gate like she's auditioning for the Kentucky Derby, arms flailing, and hollering my name as if I'm a grand prize. I half expect her to pull off a cartoonish skid, leaving skid marks that would rival a Looney Tunes character. No sign necessary to announce my awaiting status; she nearly sends me on a one-way trip into next week with her enthusiastic entrance.

"I've never been so thrilled to have my feet on solid ground. Who knew there could be so much snow? And, let me tell you about my plane buddy - she was deep into a steamy novel. I couldn't help but read over her shoulder. Now, I'm desperately in need of either a strong cocktail, or just the 'cock' part would be awesome." She manages to spill all this out in one breath while unraveling her scarf and using it as a makeshift fan.

"God, I love you," I giggle, squeezing her in a hug so tight even the air particles are exchanging high-fives.

"Where's Koti? Please tell me you brought her along?" She scans the surroundings.

"She headed to the game with my mother. She wanted to wish Jake, or as she fondly calls him, Spence, good luck in his final match before jetting off to his new team in Florida."

"I went to bed so early last night, I missed the

grand finale of the game. Jake was on a scoring spree, bagging four out of five goals," she mentions as we stroll out of the airport.

"It was his best game to date. I bet his new team is throwing a party already, but it's a major bummer for the Arctic Wolves."

"Jake moving up is like the circle of life, but for hockey. Hakuna Matata on ice," she muses.

"I adore your eternal optimism," I exclaim while wrestling her luggage into the trunk. "We've got a tight fifteen minute deadline to make it to the game before the puck drops."

"How long is the commute?" she asks, securing herself with the seatbelt like it's the last life vest on a sinking ship.

"Thirty minutes in this winter wonderland."

"Ah, the injustice that we can't teleport," she snickers.

"I wish," I chuckle back, because, honestly, avoiding traffic jams and not having to find parking? Sign me up.

"What's the latest saga with you and Jake?" she dives right in, no chill.

"Talk about sixty to zero," I mutter, easing the car into the flow of traffic and desperately wishing for that teleportation ability now.

"Are you two going to try to patch things up, or?" she probes, not one to tip-toe around a landmine.

"No," I sigh, deep. "He left with Miss Party

Favors the other night. Okay, so maybe I nudged him in her direction, and now I haven't seen or spoken to him since."

"I'm always Team You, but I'm also your personal truth bomb," she says, giving me that look that means she's going to drop me some Maggs wisdom. "You're just freaked out he'll pull a David and ghost you."

"That's what Jake said before he did his Houdini impression."

"I'm starting to like Jake's script," she grins.

"But he didn't even try to stick around. He just poofed," I grumble.

"Babe, he's probably wandering around in his own emotional fog. From the sound of it, Jake is as new to the love game as a toddler at a chess tournament. Plus, he's juggling his dream job now. That guy's internal compass must be spinning like a fidget spinner in a tornado."

Her analogy sends a laugh bubbling up from me, despite the drama. Maybe there is hope for us yet - if I can navigate through the fog and he learns to play chess, metaphorically speaking. "Okay, but let's not forget about Koti in all this mess. I mean, I can't seriously be with a man who doesn't see her as the center of his universe."

"Got it, so it's looking pretty grim for Team Jake, then."

By some stroke of cosmic luck, the traffic gods

were smiling upon us, granting us a clear path to the ice rink. We arrived with a whole sixty seconds to spare - talk about living on the edge. Thank the stars for my VIP parking spot; without it, we'd probably be circling the lot for an hour.

"Ooh, fancy ice palace," she comments as we step inside.

"I'll find Mom and Koti. You can sit with them while I work."

No sooner than Maggs steps inside the arena, Koti spots her. "Aunt Maggs!" she shrieks, launching herself down the steps like a missile with a hug as its target.

"Hey, sugar puff," Maggs greets her, picking her up.

"I've missed you. Are you going to stay with us for a while?"

"For a few days."

"Ah," she pouts. "I wish you could live with us forever."

"I hate to interrupt this reunion," I laugh, "but did you get to see Jake before the game?"

"Wait till you see what he got me," she beams, dashing off to retrieve a bag from where Mom and Seth are seated with Jewels.

"He bought me and Dorito matching jerseys for his new team, the Mango Bay Mavericks," she announces, displaying the mini-jersey.

"Oh man, if you're passing on this gem of a guy,

I'm officially in line." Maggs jests, giving me a playful jab. "That's so adorable it should be illegal. Jake's definitely playing to win, huh? Looks like he's aiming to be the MVP of Koti's heart - and maybe snag a few points with her mom too. Go Team Jake," she cheers, clapping like she's at a pep rally.

"Time for me to hustle," I say, fighting back a laugh.

Jake's all set on the ice, like a knight ready for battle, just waiting for the ref to kick things off with the puck drop. He sneaks a glance my way, and suddenly, I'm not breathing - like I've been dunked in ice water. Our eyes lock for a millisecond before he looks away, sending a shiver of coldness down my spine. What did I expect? I'm the architect of our icy divide.

The crowd's enthusiasm hits fever pitch for the Arctic Wolves, and there's Jake, turning the ice into his personal playground. My thoughts, however, decide to skate off to - let's call it the Jake Highlights - a showcase of dexterity with his hands, those award-winning maneuvers with his lips, and his unparalleled talent at making me shout his name.

"Get a grip, Piper," I scold myself, snapping out of my steamy daydream and refocusing on the actual game.

I'm in a photographic frenzy, capturing the raw intensity of the players in each shot. There's a jaw-dropping picture of Remi sending his opponent into the boards with a force that echoes through the arena. Suddenly, a member of the rival team lunges at our goalie. Jake, in a burst of fury, tosses his gloves aside like he's shedding restraints. He lands a solid blow, prompting the other guy to retaliate, locking his arms around Jake's head in a surge of aggression that propels them both to the cold, hard ice. The refs swiftly intervene, separating them and dishing out penalties, eliciting a collective hiss from the crowd.

The first period concludes with goals from Remi and Bohdi, both plays set up by Jake's slick assists. As I adjust my position for the start of the second period, the woman who left with Jake the other evening approaches me.

"You really snagged the golden puck," she comments, pressing her lips together - lips that clearly didn't shy away from a cosmetic boost.

"And how's that? You're the one playing away games with Jake," I counter, my eyebrow arching in skepticism.

"He dropped me off at my place and didn't stay. Said he's got his heart in the penalty box because of you. I even tried tempting him with a night of over-time, but he turned me down."

Her words blindside me more than a slapshot from the blue line.

"He'd sacrifice his contract for you, if you asked him to," she adds.

I spin around, my face probably looking like I've

been checked into the boards. "Did he actually say that?"

"Not explicitly, but you can see it in his eyes, like he's aiming for a goal he can't make."

"You're mistaken. And even if you weren't, I would never ask him to abandon his dreams for my sake," I retort, trying to keep my cool.

"Then you'd be a fool to not go with him," she declares, lifting her nose haughtily and swaying her hips dramatically toward where the players are about to hit the ice.

"Who was that?" Maggs materializes behind me like a curious cat.

"A walking advertisement why Jake needs a fast pass out of this town," I reply.

"Her lips - were they factory installed?" Maggs says out loud, puffing her lips out an attempt to rival the size. "Is that the blueprint for modern romance? If so, I'm about to declare myself a permanent bachelorette and start collecting cats."

"You and me both," I laugh.

"I promised Koti ice cream if it's cool with you?"

"Yeah, but let's not turn this into a sugar spree. We can't have her ricocheting off the walls like she's a pinball machine," I caution.

"Promise," she crosses her fingers behind her back as she sidesteps into the bleachers.

The second period turns into a penalty parade, with the game's intensity notching up. Jake nails a slapshot goal, and Remi doubles down, making the scoreboard a more comfortable four to two.

No one manages to sneak the puck past the goalies in the third period, securing a win for the Arctic Wolves. I gather my camera gear and join my family and Jake's still in the stands.

Maggs leans in, whispering like she's sharing state secrets, "Was I out of the loop, or did you neglect to tell me that your mom and Seth are the latest romance novel cover come to life?" They've been more tangled than headphone cords in a pocket the whole game."

"I'm just happy to witness a romantic life that's not on life-support like mine," I sigh.

Jewels wraps me in a hug and starts signing energetically.

"Jewels wants you to know that she's a big fan of yours, she really likes you, and she finds you hilarious."

"Aww, you're sweet," Maggs responds, pulling Jewels into an embrace.

"Spence!" Koti squeals, racing to the bottom of the bleachers to exchange high-fives with Jake.

My gut twists in a knot, a rollercoaster of emotions flipping and turning inside of me, seeing Jake all sweaty and ridiculously attractive in his snug white undershirt, still rocking his hockey pants. He nervously tousles his long hair, and he's gnawing on his lower lip, sending my heart into a skipping frenzy, tempting me to sprint into his arms.

Once more, Maggs leans in for a secretive chat, clutching my arm like it's the only thing holding her up. "Holy guacamole, he looks like a runway model. If you're not planning on keeping him, mind if I submit an application?" she practically drools.

As the heat index climbs south of my belly button, it's not a question of whether I want him or not. I shoot Maggs a look, urging her to pull herself together. "Your application is being denied," I mutter under my breath.

I just wrapped up the best game of my life, and my mind is solely on Piper. She thinks I slept with that woman the other night. I have to tell her nothing happened and hope she believes me. Piper has gotten a hold of my heart and won't let go. She's made it clear that we can't be together, but I can't leave things between us like this. She means too much to me.

Amidst the sea of congratulations being thrown my way, I'm searching for the one voice that really matters. There she is standing on the bleachers with my family and some unknown woman. Koti, my pint-sized cheerleader, charges toward me, hand raised for a triumphant high-five.

"Spence!" she squeals.

"Hey, cutie," I reciprocate, our hands connecting in celebration of the victory.

"My aunt Maggs is here," she points to her.

Piper's best friend. As we make our way up the bleachers hand in hand, I can't tear my eyes away from Piper.

"Great game, son," my dad congratulates with a harty slap on the back.

"Thanks, Pops."

Piper's mom leans in for a hug, and then I'm bulldozed by Jewels, signing how much she likes Piper and Maggs.

Koti wiggles between Piper and her friend.

"Hi, I'm Maggs," Piper's friend introduces herself, offering her hand. "I've heard a lot about you. And Piper wasn't fibbing - you're hot," she flings her hand away as if it just brushed a hot stove.

Piper nudges Maggs with her elbow. "Guess who's about to earn an honorary spot in the Ex-Bestie Hall of Fame?" Piper quips, talking out of the corner of her mouth.

I clear my throat, desperately trying not to burst into laughter. "Well, it's nice to meet you. Did you enjoy the game?"

"It was amazing. Congrats on your NHL contract. Before you ditch the Arctic Wolves, any chance you might hook me up with an introduction to your teammates?" she asks with a mischievous grin.

Jewels volunteers to handle the introductions, and they stroll down the bleachers arm in arm.

Koti interrupts, tugging on Piper's shirt tail. "Mommy, can I go play on the ice?"

I glance between Piper and Koti. "I was hoping we could talk before I fly out in the morning."

Piper brushes a strand of Koti's hair off of her shoulder. "I have a few hours of work to do. How about I take the entire day off tomorrow and I'll teach you some killer moves on the ice?"

"Okay," Koti cheers, giving me a hug that tugs at my heartstrings.

"I'll send you and Dorito another jersey when I get settled."

Koti squeezes me tight and kisses me on the cheek. "I love you, Spence."

My heart practically stops, and I choke back the lump in my throat. "I love you too, kiddo."

When she skips off with my dad and her grandmother, my eyes mist over and I blink several times to dry them. I turn to face Piper. "Can we go to my place to talk, where it's quiet?"

The corner of her lip draws between her teeth. "I don't know if that's such a good idea. Every time I'm alone with you, we end up in...well, you know."

I narrow the distance between us. "I haven't heard you complain," I say with a hopeful grin, attempting to ease the tension between us.

"Our,...connection, isn't the issue."

"I didn't sleep with her," I blurt out.

She runs her hand down the length of my arm. "I know. She told me how disappointed she was."

I blow out a breath I didn't realize I was holding. "So, you believe me?"

"Yes, but that doesn't change the situation between us."

"Will you please just come to my place? You can take your car and leave anytime you want."

"Maggs is in town for only a short period of time. I should go home."

"One hour. That's all I'm asking," I plead with her, channeling my inner negotiator. "Think of it as a limited-time-offer; spend sixty minutes with me, if you're not completely entertained, I'll throw in an awkward joke or two. I'm fully prepared to get on my knees, if that's what it takes."

She scratches the side of her head. "Okay, one hour, not a minute longer."

"The countdown begins the moment your beautiful self is sitting on my couch," I point a finger at her with a mock-serious expression.

"Let me go strike a deal with Maggs for Koti's bedtime tales; otherwise, we'll end up with horror stories, and Koti will be camping out in my bed. I'll rendezvous with you at your place."

"Great. I'll be there…what's that saying? With bells on? But, let's be clear, I won't be wearing any bells," I flash her a grin.

"You're such a dork," she teases.

I savor my victory as her face lights up. "I'll see you soon."

Racing to the locker room, I quickly shower and engage in final banter with some soon to be ex-team-mates. I'm really going to miss them, especially Bohdi.

"How about I take you out for one last celebration?" Bohdi offers.

"I can't. Early flight, and something I need to do before I leave."

"Piper," he states. "What's the plan with her?"

"I honestly don't know, man."

"You should cut her loose. I don't say that to be a jerk, but she deserves someone who will stick around. Your life is just kicking off, and who knows where you will end up? Chances are, it won't be in Montana."

"But what if I never find anyone like her again? I'm in love with her."

"If you truly love her, you'll leave and never look back."

I know he's right, but it's ripping me apart. "I'll shoot you a call from Florida, and if I hear any shifty business from my sister about you, I'll be back in town to kick your ass," I tease, and we share a man hug.

"Best of luck in the NHL, bro."

"Appreciate it," I reply, flinging my bag over my shoulder and hustling out to my car.

On the drive home, Bohdi's advice echoes in my mind. *"You should cut her loose."* Tonight, I had every intention of trying to keep Piper in my life, but deep down, I know she's been right all along. It's not just about her. Koti is the sweetest thing, and I don't want to break her heart along with mine. If I step away now, she's not too attached...but I certainly am to both of them.

Stepping inside, I toss my bag on the floor and make a beeline for the fridge, downing a bottle of water. Pacing around, I'm lost in my thoughts until a knock on the door jolts me.

I exhale, closing my eyes, summoning myself to do the right thing. When I open the door, all my resolve crumbles. She looks so beautiful standing in front of me, and I find myself just staring at her.

"Are you going to let me in, or did you change your mind?" she asks slowly.

"Come on in, sorry about that," I say, widening the door.

She casually shrugs out of her jacket, and I hang it on the coat rack. Without hesitation, she settles on the couch.

"Can I get you a drink?" I ask.

"No, I'm good. The clock is ticking, Jake."

I join her on the couch, drawing my leg up to face her. "I'm at a loss here. Love you and leave you - I just don't know how to pull it off."

"Jake, I..."

I gently take both her hands in mine. "Before I met you, I was a walking question mark. You helped me figure things out and get to a better place. Falling in love with you wasn't part of my plan, but here we are. I want you and hockey, but it's not that simple because it's not just about you."

She furrows her brow.

"Koti is an amazing kid, smart, and hilarious as heck. If my life were different, I'd have no doubts about where I want to be and who I'd want to be with."

"I feel the same way, and I'd never let you choose me over your dreams. You've worked tirelessly for them. Falling for you was the last thing on my agenda. When I moved here, I'd given up on the notion of falling in love again. I didn't believe I had it in me to open up my heart to someone else. You changed that for me, and I'm grateful. I want you to achieve all of your dreams. You'll meet someone and fall in love again. If there's one thing you've taught me, it's that I'm capable of letting someone else in my life. It's just a matter of whether I choose to or not. Whoever that special someone is, will have to be pretty darn extraordinary," she says, cupping my cheek.

"I don't believe I'll ever encounter someone quite like you," I rasp, kissing her until her lips are swollen." I lean back, our foreheads touching, and I gaze into her eyes. "How much longer do we have?"

"Long enough for you to make me scream your name," she grins.

Wasting no time, I scoop her up in my arms and carry her into my bedroom.

"No promises, no vows. No plans past tonight," she says softly, her cheeks flushed and her eyes dark.

I cherish the version of myself that surfaces when I'm with her. That man only exists solely when she's in my arms, and the heat in her eyes unmistakably matches mine.

"That look alone you are giving me right now could make me come," her voice sounds sexy and gritty.

"I don't have time to remove my clothes and yours. Get naked, and grab the headboard," I command, my breath as choppy as hers.

We save every second of the hour we have left, blissfully coming apart together, wave after wave. At some point, I flipped her over, and she screamed my name into my pillow. We both lie breathless not nearly done with one another, but the hour promised is up.

I roll to my back and watch her gather her clothes from the floor, making her way into my bathroom. When she shuts the door, my eyes well up with tears rolling down my cheeks. Something I hadn't done since my mother left us all those years ago. I bite my lip to keep it from trembling.

When she comes out, my chest is heavy, and it

seems like all the air is being sucked out of the room. "What if we..."

She leans down, pressing her lips to mine. "No promises, no vows, no plans past tonight," she repeats her words from earlier. "Goodbye, Jake."

22 PIPER

Four months later.

I HAVEN'T BEEN BACK to Harmony Grove since our move to Montana. It's serene, but lacks the simplicity and sheer beauty of Montana. I've grown fond of our lives in Summit Ridge, even learning to embrace the snow - it's incredible what the right gear can do. Thanks to Seth, we have everything we need, and Koti is thriving. She still talks about Jake, and it still has the power to bring tears to my eyes, some happy, some sad.

Seth and my mom are planning on tying the knot. They want to have their wedding in the middle of summer, outdoors, right in the heart of town, when Jake will be home.

Since our last night together, thoughts of him

occupy my mind every day, but I haven't spoken with him. Despite his numerous texts in the first few weeks, I refused to respond, knowing it would just hurt more in the long run.

Every game night, Jake's family and mine gather together to watch him play. He's performed exceptionally well, securing the position of leading scorer for the season, which concluded yesterday. I thought it would be the perfect time to visit Maggs in Harmony Grove.

"You're thinking about him, aren't you?" Maggs wraps her arm around my shoulder as we stroll the downtown area.

"It's hard not to," I feebly smile.

"He's not dead, you know? You could call him," Maggs suggests, attempting to boost my spirit.

"He'll be back in Summit Ridge soon enough for our parents' wedding. That sounds so weird," I snort.

"They genuinely seem happy, and Seth is a great guy. Koti adores him."

"I'm happy for them; it's just going to be challenging to see Jake."

"And by that, you mean it will be hard not to end up in his bed," she full on laughs.

"True, but I can't let that happen again. It will only make me want him more. I'm destined to be alone."

She grabs my arm, yanking me to a stop.

"Speaking of destined to be alone category," she points.

"David," I snarl, turning away to feign interest in window shopping. "Don't say anything. Maybe he won't spot us."

"Piper!" he calls my name from across the street.

"Pretend we didn't hear him," I say, keeping my tone hushed.

A car honks, and the next thing I know, I can feel him standing behind us. "Piper," he says my name again.

Reluctantly, I turn to face him. "David," I enunciate his name with my chin held high.

"It's so good to see you," he holds his arms out as if I'm expected to walk into them.

"That's not what I was thinking," I mutter.

"Me either," Maggs chimes in.

"I'd heard you moved somewhere out west with..."

"Don't say her name," I seethe, cutting him off.

"You look good," he shoves his hands in his pockets.

"Well, you look as hideous as ever," Maggs sneers, and I cover my mouth, stifling a laugh.

"Come on, don't be that way. I'm a different man now. In fact, I'd love it if you'd let me make things up to you and your daughter."

"I have no interest in you," I snap. "Your

supposed change means nothing to me. What you did is beyond forgiveness."

"I loved you. You having a child at the time meant me giving up my dreams. It wasn't my fault you chose to give up yours."

"You're a bastard!" Maggs raises her hand to smack him in the face. and I quickly snatch her wrist.

"He's not worth your energy," I grit my teeth.

"Maybe he's worth mine," a familiar voice rings out behind us.

I turn to see Jake licking an ice cream cone. "What are you doing in Harmony Grove?" Surprise colors my voice.

"I heard a beautiful woman was going to be in town," he grins.

I shoot a glare at Maggs, and she simply shrugs her shoulders.

"I'm sorry, but you're interrupting me and my girlfriend's conversation," David says.

Jake freezes, staring at me.

"He's delusional," I snicker. "Jake, I'd like you to meet David."

"David. The David," he says, nonchalantly handing his ice cream cone to Maggs. "The one that left you because you had a child?"

"That would be the one," I fold my arms over my chest.

"Who the hell are you?" David has the nerve to get ballsy with Jake.

I'm shocked when Jake extends his hand to David. "It's nice to meet you." David grips his hand in return. "I've always wanted to meet the man that handed me this gorgeous, smart, feisty woman, and her kick-ass daughter."

David narrows his eyes, looking utterly confused. "I still don't understand who you are."

"I'm the guy head over heels for her, and if you ever cross the road to so much as speak to her again, you'll be hunting for your balls on the street."

"Yeah, what he said!" Maggs gets right up in David's face.

"Easy there, girl," I chuckle.

"I don't know who the hell you think you are, but Piper is more than capable of choosing for herself!" he growls.

"She already did, you dimwit," Maggs howls.

David inches closer to me, and Jake positions himself between us like he would defend his goalie. "Tell him, Piper."

"Let's see if I can make this crystal clear," I tap a finger to my lip. "If you were the last man on earth, I wouldn't let you near me or my daughter."

"You are pond scum," Maggs adds. "Lower than pond scum."

"I think that pretty much sums it up," Jake opens and closes his hands by his side.

"Is this pretty boy with the long hair who you'd pick over me?" David spats.

"All day long," I say.

He tries to reach for me, and Jake's knee finds its place near David's crotch. "What did I tell you about your family jewels?"

David swallows hard. "Fine. You can have her and her brat." He jerks free, running across the road, nearly getting taken out by a car.

"Hey," Jake greets me with a sweet smile.

"I'm still processing that you are actually here."

"Me too," Maggs states, happily devouring Jake's ice cream.

"Help yourself," he laughs.

"Oh, you didn't give it to me to eat," Maggs scoffs teasingly.

"You flew straight here from Florida?"

"I got on the first plane out," he sweeps a piece of hair behind my ear.

"I um...forgot I have a phone call I have to make," Maggs starts backing away. "Feel free to go to my apartment. It will be available for a couple of hours, unless you need longer," she winks.

"Thanks for your help, Maggs. You're a good friend to Piper, whether she believes it or not."

"Traitor," I mouth to her, grinning.

"Lead the way," he murmurs, intertwining his fingers with mine.

"That was incredible, by the way. David had some nerve calling me his girlfriend."

"I wanted to choke him right then and there."

"Seeing him run the other way was far better."

"You were handling him just fine."

"Why exactly are you here, Jake?"

"To negotiate."

"Did you get offered another deal?" My eyes widen.

"I'll tell you all about it once we're inside."

"This is it," I say, craning my neck to look up. "She lives above a gym."

"It would be so easy to run down the stairs and work out. I'd probably do it in my boxers if I lived here."

"You'd have a line of women standing outside this window gawking at you," I playfully swat him in the chest.

"Should we head upstairs?" he asks.

We walk up the flight of stairs, and I stretch on my tiptoes to retrieve the key on the ledge above the door. "It's an open studio apartment. She moved here when we left for Montana."

"Very nice," he says, running his hand over the dark cherry-colored leather sofa.

"Do you want something to eat or drink?"

"I was enjoying an ice cream," he laughs, "but I'm good," he sits on the sofa. "Come here," he pats the spot next to him.

My body heats up as soon as our thighs touch. "You don't need me to negotiate a contract, Jake."

"I do when it involves you."

"I don't understand?" I frown.

He gets on his knees between my legs. "I want to fight for you, for Koti, for us. The NHL has been more than I could possibly have dreamt of, but it doesn't mean anything without you. When I'm not on the ice, all I think about his how much I love you. I want you and Koti to be the center of my universe."

"We've been through this, Jake. I'm not going to let you give up hockey."

"I don't have to. I want you and Koti by my side as often as possible, but even when we're not together, the two of you will still be my world." He digs a piece of paper out of his pocket, handing it to me.

"What is this? You want an actual contract with me?"

"No. Open it," he urges.

I unfold it and read it. "This is a receipt for all the medical bills showing they are paid in full," I gasp.

"If Koti were my child, I'd be responsible for all her medical needs."

"What are you saying?" tears blur my vision.

"You asked me once, what was beyond the blue line for me? That answer is you. I'm saying I want to marry you and adopt Koti."

I open my mouth to speak, and words don't come out.

"Wow, that's a first. I don't think I've ever rendered you speechless," he smirks.

I stare at him.

"Alright, now you're starting to give me a complex. Say something, Say anything."

I cup his face in my hands. "Yes," I say.

"Yes, as in you'll marry me?"

I nod, tears streaming down my face.

"Thank God. I had this whole plan worked out to kidnap you and hold you hostage until you said yes," he wipes the back of his hand across his forehead.

"And, what exactly were you going to do to me to convince me to say yes?" I raise a single eyebrow.

He stands, offering me his hand. "Where's the bedroom, and I'll show you? Don't worry; the kidnapping plot was just for dramatic effect," he says, wrapping his arms around me.

"You can still show me what you had in mind, right?" I tease, licking my lips and fixating on his mouth.

"Every. Single. Naughty. Detail," he tosses me over his shoulder.

EPILOGUE

What a rollercoaster of a year it's been! My mom and Seth are now happily hitched, gallivanting around the globe like travel-hungry lovebirds. I swear, if they were any happier, they'd be floating on clouds made of cotton candy.

And here I am, gazing out the window of our swanky new pad, reveling in the brilliance of my decision to tie the knot with the cocky, Adonis-like jock, Jake. He's out there constructing a treehouse for Koti, with her adorable little self sporting a matching tool belt, probably causing more chaos than construction. But hey, he's got the patience of a saint. Koti adores him, and he treats her like she's the queen of the treehouse realm. They're like two mischievous peas in a pod.

Sure, Jake's jetting off with his team all the time, but we tag along whenever we can. I was even offered a gig as a social media manager for an NHL team, but I was like, "Nah, I'll pass." Who needs the NHL when you've got a hubby who showers you with flowers and has your best friend on speed dial for those moments when you need some top-notch girl time? Not me, that's for sure!

Speaking of surprises, it's my turn to pull a rabbit out of the hat. I'm about to drop the bombshell on Jake that we're expanding our little clan. I never knew I could love someone as much as I love that man. Life may not always follow the script you had in mind, but in my case, it's turned out to be a wild, wonderful ride that's exceeded all my wildest dreams.

KEEP READING for the first chapter of Two Years Without You.

SNEAK PEEK AT TWO YEARS
WITHOUT YOU

Two Years Without You

BESTSELLING AUTHOR
KELLY MOORE

"I love you both dearly, and I'll miss you." Magnolia, Nola for short, wraps her arms around my neck, squeezing tight, as Sully tugs at her hand.

"You always hog all of Mom's hugs," he scowls.

Releasing Nola with one hand and opening my arms, he joins our embrace. "There is always room for one more."

Eight years ago, I was shouting, "release the krakens!" from my belly, and their dad's hand was the emergency exit lever. I'm starting to suspect that they are secret time travelers who skipped a few years, full of wisdom and mischief.

"Kiss," I say, puckering my lips and pressing them to their cheeks, one at a time. "I want you both to be good and well-behaved for Grandma and Grandpa while I'm gone."

With a theatrical flair, Sullivan, the eye-roller

extraordinaire, declares, "we will," as he sends his big gray eyes on a thrilling, gravity-defying roller-coaster ride, putting on a spectacle of bravery for his sister that could rival any action hero.

"Call me every day." Nola's eyes start to well up.

"You'll be having so much fun at the beach you'll hardly have time to miss me." I gently stroke my palm down her dark, chocolate-colored braid.

"It's time for you to board the plane, sweetheart." My mother cups my cheek. "Try not to worry. Your father and I will take good care of them and keep them busy while you're gone."

"I'm not worried, but I'll miss them like crazy. Perhaps I should only be gone a week or two rather than all summer." My eyes tear up.

"You need this, and so do they. It's time. It's been two years since Danny passed away, and you haven't returned to visit his family. It's wonderful that they're hosting a party in his memory. Joey has extended an invitation to you every year, and it's time you go. I've witnessed you tending to everyone else's needs except your own since Danny died, and you could really benefit from the break."

"I don't know what I would've done without you and Dad to help me with the twins after Danny died." I hug her.

They flew to my house as fast as they could after my husband's tragic death and convinced me to move to Florida with them, leaving Idaho and all the memories of Danny behind. It was the best thing I could do for the kids at the time. Their father was gone, and Evan walked out of our lives. I felt so alone. Leaving seemed like the only solution to get through our grief.

"Don't give it a minute's thought. We'd do anything for our daughter and grandkids."

As the final boarding call echoes, I embrace them once more. "I love you," I say. Stepping back, I pull my suitcase along, blow them a kiss, and wipe away the tears pooling in my eyes. I scan my ticket and take one last glance over my shoulder before I board the plane.

Locating my window seat, I stow my carry-on in the overhead compartment and navigate past the other two passengers seated in my row. Both are already engrossed in their own worlds, with earbuds in place. As I settle into my seat and secure my seat belt, I gaze out the compact window. The plane begins its ascent, and soon, I find myself surrounded by a sea of white billowy clouds.

My mind drifts back to the first time I met Danny and Evan.

HALF BROTHERS, but bonded as family by heart. It had only been a few weeks since I'd relocated to Meridian for a teaching job, and I found myself strolling through a charming downtown area during a fall farmers market. A beautiful piece of artwork grabbed my attention, but given my modest teacher's salary, I couldn't afford it. The artist behind the painting had me cornered, trying to persuade me how nice it would look in my apartment. As I attempted my elegant retreat, I backed into an unmovable force of nature, inadvertently crushing a set of toes. "I'm so sorry," I stammered, my gaze locking onto the most captivating pair of charcoal-gray eyes, as rare as a unicorn sighting, surrounded by eyelashes even Rapunzel would envy.

In response, the victim of my footsie faux pas, with lips so perfect they could make a supermodel blush, uttered, "You're welcome to use my toes as your personal dance floor any day."

I couldn't help but burst into laughter, though it came out as more of a snort, and not the dainty, charming kind. More like a cross between a goose honk and a hiccup. If that didn't send him running, I figured I had just found my lifelong dance partner.

Pretending to strain my ears, I said, "I don't hear any music playing. Do you?"

He turned his attention to me, his eyes doing a delightful tango across my figure. "I believe you and I could be the composers of our own musical masterpiece."

As tempting as that sounded, the thought of me busting a move in front of a crowd seemed more likely to make him spring to the foothills than into my arms.

"How about you let me make amends by treating you to one of those mouth-watering fried donuts." I pointed to the sign and the line of people.

He swiveled his head toward the food truck and then back at me, scratching the side of his beard and crinkling his nose. "Do you think they've got gooey chocolate ones?"

"Gooey," I howl. "They're fried. I think gooey is their middle name," I said, adding air quotes for emphasis.

"Are you making fun of me?" He sported a smug grin, and my insides did a dance of their own.

"That would be rude of me," I smirked. "So, do you want one or not?"

"I'd be a fool to not let you make amends for the great *toe*tastrophe." He nodded, motioning for me to follow him.

"That's a bit of an exaggeration, don't you think?" I playfully winked, gazing up at his devastatingly handsome face.

We stopped when we reached the end of the line, and he stuck out his hand. "I'm Evan Monroe."

"Maeve Thomason," I introduced myself, slipping my hand into his, feeling like it was right where it belonged. I paused to savor the sight of him, allowing my gaze to linger as if caught in a leisurely stroll, unfazed by rush hour traffic. He stood at least six feet tall, and his hair matched the hue of the donut he seemed eager to order, complete with a well-suited beard and mustache. The word brawny came to mind. I had never been particularly drawn to bearded men, but it looked incredibly sexy on him. The gray beanie he wore seemed to echo the color of his eyes. Even beneath the layers of his flannel shirt he had rolled up to his mid-bicep, I could sense there was a muscular body underneath, one that made my lips curl with delight.

"Mae. I like it," he said with a coy smile so wide it could have doubled as a billboard. "How about we cap off this meet-cute with a coffee date? We can dive deeper into your charming klutziness and the monumental moment when you crushed my dance dreams." His mischievous expression complemented his already devastatingly good looks, like a cherry on top of a gorgeous sundae.

In the bustling circus of my mind, eight out of ten voices were waving red flags, desperately trying to convince me that this idea was pure lunacy. One voice was in the corner, drumming her fingers and suspiciously eyeing the situation, and then there was the tenth voice, the rogue one, just casually humming along to its own beat. It was the rebellious tenth voice that made me blurt out, "I'd love to."

He had charisma for days, and our playful banter was like a never-ending sitcom, complete with laugh tracks and witty one-liners. For the first time since I'd relocated to Idaho, I felt a sense of happiness and optimism about my future, instead of the initial apprehension that gripped me when I moved three thousand miles away from the only place I had ever called home.

I had to summon my inner Zen master to prevent myself from giving in to the tantalizing temptation to swipe the delicious-looking chocolatey smudge from the corner of his mouth...with my tongue.

As we took our seats, a man's voice rang out, calling his name, and he skillfully maneuvered his way through the crowd of people in the small area. "Evan!"

He waved him over. "This is my brother, Danny Archer."

Danny didn't divert his gaze from me as he pulled out the chair between us. He sported a distinct look compared to Evan, a clean-shaven face and the all-American boy next door appearance that would attract any woman's attention. His eyes were a mesmerizing shade of green with flecks of gold, and the only resemblance they shared was their height and body structure.

"Maeve," I replied as he gently kissed my knuckles.

"Where in the world did you come from?" he asked, his face lighting up.

"I just moved here a few weeks ago from Florida."

"Did you descend from the pearly gates, or did they have a clearance sale up in heaven?" He scooted his chair closer, ready to charm his way into our conversation.

"She's a teacher," Evan chimed in, recalling our earlier conversation while waiting in line for donuts.

"And what is your line of work?" My question was more directed at Evan, but Danny took over the conversation.

"I'm an adventure guide for an outdoor company, primarily leading fishing tours."

"That sounds exciting."

"Boring compared to this one." He hiked a thumb over his shoulder. "He's a smokejumper."

"Wow, that sounds like a thrilling and dangerous job."

He opened his mouth to respond, but Danny interjected, "He's never home. Always out some-where fighting fires."

I squinted. "You two are brothers?"

"Half brothers," Danny clarified. "We share the same mother."

"My old man passed away when I was two." Evan's gaze fell to his hands that were folded on the table.

"I'm so sorry to hear that. That must have been very difficult for you and your mother."

"I don't really remember much about him."

"So, your mom remarried?"

"She was remarried within a year and had Danny, then Joey three years later."

"And you're all three very close?"

"Best friends," Danny replied, giving his brother a playful slap on the shoulder. "What about you? Do you have any siblings?"

"No. I'm an only child."

"Well, that's a silver lining because this guy is a certified professional pain in my ass." Danny erupted into laughter, echoing like a burst of fireworks.

Danny oozed charm like a honey jar—sweet and impossible to handle without making a sticky mess.

Coffee led to dinner and a few drinks, with plenty of conversation in between. I enjoyed their company, but my attention kept gravitating to Evan. He was more reserved than Danny and seemed to have bitten his lip a few times, allowing his brother to dominate most of the conversation.

At one point, Danny caught Evan and me gazing at one another. "Evan, I could use another drink," he announced, rising from his seat. "How about you?"

"I'll have a beer," Evan replied, raising his glass.

"Great, you can join me," Danny suggested, tilting his head toward the bar.

"Oh, alright." Evan frowned but stood to follow his brother.

I admired Evan's backside as he walked away and then leaned against the bar with one elbow and turned to the side to face Danny. I sipped my drink, observing the two of them engaged in a hushed conversation just out of earshot. Evan glanced at me, then back at Danny, his jaw firmly set. It was evident that he wasn't pleased with the discussion, but I was never privy to its contents. All I could discern was that when Danny and Evan returned to the table, things were different. Evan's demeanor had turned cool, and he avoided making eye contact with me. Thirty minutes later, he excused himself and didn't return.

Danny, on the other hand, was like a detective on a mission to unravel the enigma that was me. With the charm of a smooth-talking diplomat and good looks that could rival a movie star's, I was genuinely enjoying my time with him.

Danny was unrelenting in his pursuit, and we began dating. However, whenever I saw Evan while we were together, I couldn't help but wonder if he was the one I was meant to be with. That is until he began bringing other women around me. Three months later, I professed my love to Danny, finally pushing thoughts of Evan out of my mind.

Another three months passed, and I found myself strolling down the aisle, taking the name Maeve Archer. I briefly hesitated when I saw Evan in a tuxedo, standing beside his brother as his best man. As I approached the altar, I could see a look of longing. He swallowed hard and closed his eyes, shoving his hands deep into his pockets, seemingly trying to shake it off. When he opened them again, a sense of detachment had settled between us.

During the reception, I discovered a bathroom upstairs in the old house, complete with a clawfoot tub. I was in the middle of applying a layer of lipstick when I heard the wooden floor creaking in the hallway coming closer and the sound of Evan's voice. In a moment of panic, I swiftly lifted my white gown and slipped into the bathtub, pulling the curtain closed around it. It's puzzling why I didn't simply reach over to lock the door or leave, but my heart raced, and all I could do was hide.

Evan's speech was slurred when he opened the door, and a woman's voice followed him inside. The door closed, and the next thing I heard was the sound of heavy breathing mixed with a rhythmic slapping noise that could only be the sound of skin against skin. I couldn't help but gasp, quickly covering my mouth with my hand to stifle the sound.

The encounter lasted a mere five minutes before the woman's heels clacked against the floor. "That was fun," she remarked before walking out.

Evan released a sigh and turned on the water. I could barely make out his words as he spoke, "If only it were the woman I truly wanted."

After turning off the water, he stumbled out of the bathroom, with the sound of him zipping up his pants in the background.

At that moment, I wondered who he might be

talking about. I had witnessed him with numerous women since the night we first met. It was quite evident he had no romantic interest in me; he had kept his distance, and his acknowledgment usually came in the form of a snide remark. I never managed to pinpoint what might have turned him away, not that it truly mattered. I was head over heels in love with Danny, and just moments ago, I had become his wife. Any lingering doubts, I buried deep within my heart, vowing never to revisit them again. Danny was now my life, and I promised to love him until death do us part.

AS I LEAN BACK against the seat, a rush of more memories floods my mind, some heartwarming and others deeply saddening. I never thought I'd find myself able to relate to Evan, who lost his father when he was only two years old. My kids were six when they lost their dad, and I often wonder how much of him they will remember as they grow older. He loved them, but there were moments when I sensed an unexplainable sadness in him.

We had spent a year trying to conceive without success. Danny was resolved to it being just the two of us for the rest of our lives, and he was content with that. I, on the other hand, insisted on both of us undergoing testing, and it turned out Danny was sterile. He again made it clear that all we needed was each other, but I couldn't give up on the dream of having children. I delved into researching sperm donors, and eventually, Danny finally agreed if it was going to make me happy. Twins were never part of the plan, but I'm grateful we had two because Danny didn't want any more children.

The sound of the airplane's wheels lowering for their landing position brings me back to the present.

Little did I anticipate that eight years later, I would find myself a widow with the sole responsibility of raising our twins.

ABOUT THE AUTHOR

"This author has the magical ability to take an already strong and interesting plot and add so many unexpected twists and turns that it turns her books into a complete addiction for the reader." Dandelion Inspired Blog

Armed with books in the crook of my elbow, I can go anywhere. That's my philosophy! Better yet, I'll write the books that will take me on an adventure.

My heroes are a bit broken but will make you swoon. My heroines are their own kick-ass characters armed with humor and a plethora of sarcasm.

If I'm not tucked away in my writing den, with coffee firmly gripped in hand, you can find me with a book propped on my pillow, a pit bull lying across my legs, a Lab on the floor next to me, and two kittens running amuck.

My current adventure has me living in Idaho with my own gray-bearded hero, who's put up with my shenanigans for over thirty years, and he doesn't mind all my book boyfriends.

If you love romance, suspense, military men, lots of action and adventure infused with emotion, tear-worthy moments, and laugh-out-loud humor, dive into my books and let the world fall away at your feet.

Follow me on Tiktok and Instagram @kelly-mooreauthor.com

Book 1

Book 2

Book 3

Printed in Great Britain
by Amazon